Wildlife on Co

Devina Sivagurunathan

Shivani Sivagurunathan is a Malaysian fiction writer and poet. Born in Kuala Lumpur and raised in Port Dickson, she spent eight years in the UK, where she studied Comparative Literature. She lives in Malaysia and lectures at Universiti Putra Malaysia.

Wildlife on Coal Island

Stories

SHIVANI SIVAGURUNATHAN

HarperCollins *Publishers* India

First published in 2011 by Universiti Putra Malaysia Press
First published in India in 2012 by
HarperCollins *Publishers* India
Building 10, Tower A, 4th Floor, DLF Cyber City, Phase II,
Gurugram Haryana – 122002, India
www.harpercollins.co.in

1 2 3 4 5 6 7 8 9 10

P-ISBN: 978-93-5029-353-9
E-ISBN: 978-93-5029-537-3

Typeset in 11/14 Venetian301 BT at
SURYA

Printed and bound at
MicroPrints India, New Delhi

For my parents

Contents

Preface

THE STORIES IN this collection emerged, as most stories do, from a solitary space, one that every writer needs in order to let her creations come to life. Ironically, it is through that aloneness that the plural voices of the imagination spring into acoustic prominence. One might even say that in the thick silence of dawn, as a writer prepares to enter an as yet unknown world, the stories are fine-tuning their strings, producing a din (melodious or otherwise), somewhere inside the self's system. With a book like *Wildlife on Coal Island* that internal noise was especially complex since the characters that inhabit this fictional island are many and diverse. So it transpired that working on this collection was a paradoxical experience, at once deeply reclusive and active where the characters' dictation could only come into being in physical quietude.

The creation of Coal Island was a simple but long-germinating reaction to having grown up in a small town in Malaysia in the 1980s and '90s. Before the Internet became a presence in households, before the advent of iPhones, iPods, iPads, and particularly in a town that had little to offer a child in need of entertainment, observing and listening seemed to be inevitable tools in the quest for making life not simply liveable but, more importantly, thrilling. Thus, looking and hearing became toys – malleable ones – that brought about a whole host of other people's adventures and also, because we lived by the sea and amidst vegetation teeming with life, of the natural world. It is by no accident that the inhabitants of Coal Island carry out their days in relation to the animals and plants that surround them. There seemed to be a subtle process that existed in which the flora and fauna, often taken for granted as part of the landscape, made their way into the lives of people. They possess not merely symbolic roles but manifest their function literally as well. The 'wildness', the 'otherness' of the natural world, at times disconcerting for human beings, also, I believe, resides within us – in moments so strange to us when the self sheds its certainty under the influence of duress and desperation. The stories here, then, are the result of years of watching and listening, of seeing the relationships that occur between one person and another, between people and meaningful monkeys, interfering bats or pesky pythons. Ultimately, the external sounds and sights and stories that floated through the town in which I grew up, which were taken to be mere amusements at one time, transfigured into the pandemonium of the imagination that happily coexisted with the silence at dawn which is also the silence of childhood in a small town, if I am permitted to think in terms of a continuum of experience.

Serdang, 2011 SHIVANI SIVAGURUNATHAN

Acknowledgements

I WOULD LIKE to thank Paul McGregor for visually creating Coal Island, and for reading the stories and contributing his insights and criticisms which have helped to enliven the stories.

My sincerest appreciation goes to Arijit Sen and Ajitha G.S. for having faith in this collection.

Also, I am grateful to Tammy Ho Lai-Ming and Jeff Zroback for publishing two stories from this book, 'The Bat Whisperer' and 'Catching Iguanas', in their wonderful literary magazine, *Cha: An Asian Literary Journal*.

Thank you to my parents and my sister Devina for being a part of Coal Island, for listening about people who didn't exist for them but who did for me and were, therefore, magically, a reality for us all.

Finally, my warmest regards to the Coal Islanders. You have begun a world that spins even in moments of repose.

1

All About the Monkey

I HAVE LIVED on Coal Island my whole life, a total of twenty-five years and eleven months. The island is 150 square miles in area and my favourite fact about it is that unlike other parts of Malaysia, Coal Island doesn't produce red watermelons, only the yellow kind. Don't ask me why. Maybe that's part of its charm. For those who insist on red watermelons, we have them imported from the mainland but they generally taste less exciting than ours. Some people even believe that red watermelons are injected with syrup. Those who eat red watermelons on the island also belong to a type. They are the lost ones, the non-natives who have somehow found their way here, now thoroughly swallowed and digested by time. They will say things like, 'Back in the day when I lived in a bungalow in Kuala Lumpur . . .' or 'You know I used to be a big, big businessman in the city'. They are listened to but not taken terribly seriously.

The truth is that although I've been encouraged by well-wishers to leave, I don't think I ever need to, a conviction I arrived at a few days ago after my encounter with a cinema-owner's widow and her monkey.

During the first few days after the cinema-owner's death his wife was found sitting in her garden with packets of winter melon tea, talking to visiting kingfishers and her resident frogs. That's the thing about Coal Island. We have plenty of people like Choong Li who don't mind you watching them doing things they should be doing in secret. After her husband's death, a natural question moved from house to house: What will happen to the cinema? We hoped that if Choong Li was a true Chinese then she would mourn for a decent amount of time and subsequently pay tribute to her husband in the form of running the business. Unfortunately for us, Choong Li chose to channel her husband's spirit through the local medium, Mrs Mano, and she had clear instructions from him that she had no right to touch what was once his and that to remind her of his humiliating death, she should get a pet monkey.

At some point every day, Choong Li would scream out the monkey's name and ask it, 'You love mummy or not?' Moments later we would hear Choong Li cooing, pacifying the simian who we soon gathered had gone into an inexplicable infant rage and eaten a row of chrysanthemums in her garden. But Choong Li, even though she shouted, was never angry at Mee Lan and could be seen sitting the monkey down on a garden stool, saying, 'Mee Lan ah, you cannot do like that. You must always have logic. Why the flowers? Why they must take your anger? Ah, if you ask like that, then you won't kill the flowers.' We never expected Mee Lan to understand the true meaning of those words but it had to be said that her behaviour improved as the days went by. For instance, every morning Mee Lan was seen picking up dead leaves from Choong Li's front porch and carefully collecting them in an orange plastic bag before tying and throwing it into the large skip down the road. Then we would see them having tea in the garden (Mee Lan nursed a bottle of milk) while Choong Li read the newspapers to Mee Lan who seemed to listen. There were days when I thought that soon enough we would see Mee Lan taking notes and engaging in discussions with Choong Li and if that day ever happened Coal Island would finally be on the map. Imagine the Guinness Book of World Records photographing Choong Li and Mee Lan: 'Coal Island produces world's first talking monkey'. Fame, fortune and fantastic fiasco would follow for us all. People would come from as far away as Iceland to see what God had given to the citizens of Coal Island and they would say, 'Lucky bastards. If only we had a talking animal to make us special.' We'd have to protect ourselves from potential thieves and the island's perimeters would be studded with big fat men with guns. We'd be safe and rich and envied.

But Mee Lan never learned how to write or speak. Despite this I still felt that there was something latent within the monkey. The way she looked at the world as though she were classifying each object into clever categories made me think that she would speak up one day and when she did we'd learn all about the mysteries of life. I made it a point to go on daily walks past Choong Li's house so that I could track the monkey's progress.

'Kumar, everyday walking only. Trying to lose weight, ah?' asked Mrs Teng one day when she saw me taking slow steps towards the house of (perhaps) the world's first talking monkey. I stopped to chat with her so that my talent-spotting wouldn't be detected, making me seem like a legitimate walker and an interested neighbour.

'Cheh, you think I need to lose weight?' I replied.

'No lah, just asking only. So, what you have been up to?'

'Same thing lah, Auntie. But I think they'll be making me manager soon.'

'Wahwah. Then you become bigshot. Make sure you don't forget Auntie when I come there to eat, okay?'

'Of course lah, Auntie.'

Just as Mrs Teng was about to reply we heard Choong Li begin her daily screaming of Mee Lan's name and the speedy quelling of that with her murmurings of deep affection. 'Oh yes, Mummy loves you too, oh yes, Mummy loves you too.'

'Where got people like this?' Mrs Teng said.

'But, Auntie, why you say that?'

Mrs Teng looked at me as though I had asked her to kill somebody for me.

'Not good you know people behave like this. It's mean, something upstairs not right.'

'But, Auntie, it only means she loves her pet.'

'Hah! So young, so innocent. How old you now ah, boy?'

She was looking at me with some kind of spite in her eyes.

Perhaps she hated all young things, Mee Lan included.

'Not so young anymore lah, Auntie. Twenty-five years old already.'

'Hah! Twenty-five only. But still. When I was twenty-five Sin Yee pop out of me. Eh, you don't know what people say about her and the monkey?'

The eyes were getting deeper and the spite was becoming bolder. It was hard to look at them especially when I compared them to Mee Lan's eyes which were full of clear, fuss-free curiosity.

'Sorry, Auntie, don't know. People are happy she found a friend after Uncle, I mean, her husband's death, isn't it?'

'First first, of course lah. Then she really start behave like one mad woman. Monkey is monkey, Kumar, human is human.'

I wanted to excuse myself and carry on with my walk but I felt that she hadn't really answered my question.

'Yes, but people are happy she found a friend, right?'

'Kumar, you tell me what kind of friend is this monkey?'

'Don't know.'

'Hai, still a boy,' she said, shaking her head like one of those dolls that can vibrate even when someone breathes on it. 'Let Auntie tell you something. Got people in this world who do evilness.'

'What do you mean?'

'People say,' she whispered, 'Choong Li and Mee Lan more than friends, you know.'

'Chik, Auntie, chik chik!'

'Got true one. You wait and see. One of these days we all be invited to one wedding.'

In that moment I knew I couldn't stand to listen to her any longer, visualizing as I walked away, the matrimonial practicalities of a human and monkey union. I forgot all about my plans to discover the world's first talking monkey and devised a new one instead. I would find my way into Choong Li's house and see for myself if a new kind of love had been invented. I wasn't sure if she would welcome me in because lonely people can be erratic sometimes. They could have either arrived at a point of complete boredom with themselves or when they had grown so attached to their routines that they resorted to sourness or terrorism if someone tried to interfere with how they chose to exist. (I heard that old Mr Percy who lived alone in his hilltop mansion threw coconuts at a pair of Jehovah's Witnesses when they tried to tell him that Jehovah could save his cataract eyes).

I knew that Choong Li wasn't the sort of person to be seduced by fruit. If I had been an ordinary spy I would've brought along a basket of mangosteens, durians and rambutans – the best of tropical fruits – and hoped to be let in for my kindness. But I knew that Choong Li would have preferred something with more depth, something that would remain for a longer time than plucked fruits. I brought along a handful of guava seeds that Mrs Mano had given me for picking out fleas on her cat, Mr Raju.

I rang the bell and waited. I suppose Choong Li was surprised to hear it and I was shocked that it even worked, seeing that it hadn't been used in a while. Mee Lan appeared and looked at me from behind the gate. A few times she reached out for the padlock and pretended to unlock it while

I looked on in hope but whenever she saw me smile, she retreated until finally I grabbed the key from her hands and let myself in. Mee Lan screeched and within seconds Choong Li was shouting, 'What has happened to Mummy's precious? What has happened to Mummy's precious?'

Then she saw me. At first I thought she was going to fling Mee Lan at me and the creature would scratch at my face until there was nothing left but before she could I held out my hand and said, 'Here, Auntie, I brought you some seeds. Guava.' She picked Mee Lan up and carried her like a baby, looking at my seeds with suspicion and admiration.

'Why you suddenly bringing Auntie gifts? What you want?'

'Nothing. Just that I saw you have a mango tree and I thought you might like a guava tree too.'

'Plenty of people here have mango trees,' she said, holding Mee Lan up as a shield as if I held any power to attack her.

'I know but they can get seeds any time. You are always at home so I thought I would save you a trip out. These are special seeds you know, Auntie. Tree will grow big and strong and the fruits will be the best on Coal Island.'

I'm not sure if it was what I said, the tone in my voice or the fact that she was probably lonely, but after I spoke, Choong Li let go of Mee Lan and the monkey, as if she knew exactly what her owner wanted, opened the front door and ushered me into the hall.

The house was the cleanest house I had ever seen. The floor shone, reflecting the ceiling and even the air smelled as though it had been washed. It's funny because I always imagined Choong Li's house to be strewn with monkey toys, banana skin and old newspapers decorated with gossamer.

'Wah, Auntie, your house so clean,' I said. She watched me closely, a bit flattered, I suspected, and my heart fluttered because I saw that the monkey was approaching me. I began to think of all the things it would do to me. Chew on my toes. Play at my face. Bite and infect me with some simian disease.

'Mee Lan, the boy is not a toy,' Choong Li said, 'Come back to Mummy.' The monkey returned to her lap and the two watched me as I looked back at them, wondering what I should say. Should I ease quietly into getting an answer or should I just tell her what people have been saying about the kind of love she's created with her monkey? There was no real need for that because she soon started talking while Mee Lan sat coolly on her lap, staring ahead as if she knew more than most monkeys.

'Eh, you're a special boy, you know, for ringing my bell. All this time, I was waiting for someone brave to do that. After all, if you think about it, what did I do? Am I a witch? No. Am I a murderer? Not really. What has actually happened?' she said, her eyes on mine.

Was she expecting a reply? Or was it one of those rhetorical questions? But it wasn't clear what had actually happened. I nodded.

'That's right. Aiyah, it's a twist of fate lah. He died like a monkey. Then he's replaced by a monkey. How you think it all happened?' She paused.

I am not a psychic, I wanted to say, but she had obviously not meant for that question to be answered. I nodded.

'That's right. That's right.' She played with Mee Lan's fur

and looked at me but she wasn't really looking at me, more like looking past me, through me. What was right? Nothing had been answered.

'Now I can be a real woman. Don't think nasty things, okay? I'm not *grateful* that he's dead. You see how I comb Mee Lan's hair? I bathe her, feed her, scold her. Anyone will say that I'm a good wife. But this time it's better. You know why? Aiyah, no more secrets lah, Kumar. Mee Lan doesn't slap me, or hit me hard when she doesn't like something. She only screams in a corner.'

I thought about her husband who had been a silent kind of man with a puffy, marshmallow face and soft, fat hands which had been felt by everybody on Coal Island when they handed him their cinema tickets. I couldn't imagine those hands delivering anything quick or hard since they were slow and soft. But because Choong Li's face suddenly became oval and white when she referred to her dead husband, I believed that their life as a married couple had been like what most people said matrimonial units were meant to be: tiring and full of guilt.

My first visit was restricted to the hall area, mainly because Choong Li's monologue determined that I could be no Columbus even though my eyes travelled to every corner in her pale green room which was littered with a mixture of random ornaments. I spotted three laughing Buddhas, fat, lively and chipped. There were also numerous toads, some olive coloured, some brown as though they had been dipped in mud, each one carrying a single coin in its mouth. In and around them were ducks of many sizes as well as little

Chinese dolls with bright white faces and deep red mouths. There was nothing beautiful about the hall but I admitted to myself as my eyes landed on those badly arranged objects that somehow, together, they held some kind of appeal.

As she spoke I realized that Choong Li's story not only answered the most basic curiosities that the neighbourhood had about her life but that it was also an obvious tale. It was no secret that she had been the typical unhappy small-town wife who worked for her husband and was therefore exempted from providing friendly customer service. I remember the time when she got into a fight with Mrs Rosli who had asked her a simple question as she was buying snacks before entering the cinema, 'Is your food halal?' Choong Li had somehow taken offence to this and spat in Mrs Rosli's face saying, 'Eh, you people think you're so clean ah?' Minutes later Choong Li was violently grabbing at Mrs Rosli's *tudung* and the two indulged in the first and so far only public physical female fight on Coal Island. When Choong Li's husband heard the commotion he stepped forth sadly and said in an equally sad voice, 'Li ah, come inside. Got customer waiting to buy ticket.' And this was the man who had supposedly delivered quick hard slaps on his fighter wife? It seemed to me that there were many underground things in this household, way before the appearance of Mee Lan who, I decided, was the logical conclusion to whatever else had happened in the past.

I returned home that day, knowing that as I walked, curtains were opened and eyes were watching me, not so secretly, from bedrooms and kitchens and halls. Mee Lan, I realized, wasn't really the hero or curiosity of Choong Li's story although to the rest of the world she was and until I found out more I too would maintain this when the nosy people of Coal Island asked me innumerable questions which I knew would come sooner than I would have liked. The first came from my parents who I found sitting in our garden with tight, unimpressed faces. 'So Kumar,' my father said, 'not enough that you shame us and refuse to go to university. Now you want to become the local gossip, prancing around, swinging your bum like a girl and openly going into that pariah's house? Tell me, what all did you learn in there? That she's sharing a bed with her monkey? That soon we will see one human–monkey baby? You know what all people are saying and still you have no shame. I don't know what kind of son I have given life to.'

My mother, as she always did, tried to pacify him and, as always, failed. Ever since I scored straight A-s in the STPM exam and refused to further my studies my father turned dark and said things like, 'Look at how shiny the bloody bum's shoes are. Have you ever seen a man wearing shoes like that?' Or, 'He walks like a seasoned prostitute.' My mother watched on and attempted to appease him with a, 'Papa, leave him alone,' but the words fell flat on the ground and on his ears.

Life at home had become a very lonely business for me as I spent most of my time in my room, reading books like *Gulliver's Travel, The Ultimate Guide to Geology* and *Hamlet* (possibly my favourite book). If I had gone to university, I'd probably have read out the entire library. But so what? Life was not created to be spent at study cubicles and lecture halls but out in the open, in the muck and grease of the world, in the soot and secrets of Coal Island, in a restaurant visited by all sorts of characters.

But my father didn't see things the way I did. 'Imagine,' he would tell me, 'what people will say when they hear you're a great big doctor, lawyer or engineer. You'll be the one to pull our family up to the heavens and we can look down at the whole world and make my Papa and Amma proud.'

When my father confronted me upon my return from Choong Li's house I looked at him and said, 'Appa, people matter, you know.' He immediately rose from his seat and held out a fist, threatening, at last, to throw that punch which had been looming in our relationship for years. It didn't come. My father, the Coward. My father, the castrated Professor of Manliness. All he had were threats which weren't even scary to begin with. I walked past him, bowing before the invisible fist, and stayed in my room, forgoing dinner and any further communication with my family. I spent the night thinking about Choong Li and why it was that we didn't know much about her life apart from the plain facts of her dissatisfaction as a wife and her desperation as a widow. I imagined her life with her husband as a collection of aggravated moments that were tinged with frustration, anger and lust, both parties refusing to succumb to the other's needs yet knowing that at some point they would have to meet in a mutual space which was most readily available in bed. The situation made me think of clogged pipes.

On my cycle to work the next day I was stopped once

again by Mrs Teng who I suspected had been waiting for me to pass by because she ran out to stand in front of my bicycle so that I braked spontaneously and almost fell. She laughed, an unfair, unkind sort of laugh, and didn't apologize. 'Kumar ah,' she said, 'next time more careful lah.' I ignored her and started preparing to leave but she said, 'Wait,' and I, always the polite, nervous type, did so.

'Everyone talking about your visit to our good neighbour house,' she giggled, 'what happen lah?'

The desire in her voice for delicious old-fashioned gossip appealed to me because I understood such urges and needs but I thought about the marriage of clogged pipes and Choong Li's oval white face and felt that I should be the only one to have that knowledge.

I said, 'Her house is very clean, Mrs Teng.'

She squinted, her giggling curtailed by her surprise at my refusal to reveal details of what she believed to be the moral disintegration of an unhappy widow.

'I see. What else, boy?'

I hated that she called me boy as if all that summed me up was my Adam's apple.

'There are also a lot of ducks in the hall.'

Mrs Teng's eyes grew big. I could tell she was getting interested. Her face stretched and was giving way to a satisfied smile.

'I see. I see. So the crazy woman keeping duck *and* monkey. I must tell Jessie Foong.'

She looked around with an expression on her face that suggested she was conducting a dangerous, mafia activity.

'Other than duck?' she whispered.

'Other than ducks there are also toads.'

She gasped and coughed and inhaled from her asthma pump. 'How many?'

'Too many to count.'

'Some more, some more?'

'Oh and this one Choong Li told me in confidence. She said she also has a laughing Buddha staying in her house.'

After another suck from her pump, Mrs Teng said, 'The woman really gone cuckoo. She think Buddha living with her. Eh, thanks boy. You really help Auntie today.'

And that was how I, directly or indirectly, confirmed the false rumours about Choong Li's mental health. Technically, I hadn't lied. There were after all ducks and toads and three laughing Buddhas in her house. To tell the truth, I allowed those rumours to float around the neighbourhood so that I could protect Choong Li from them knowing about the actual depths of her life which they would never understand anyway.

That day after I had been told that I wasn't going to become the manager of 'Good Life Western Food' I visited Choong Li. Mee Lan let me in and offered me a banana as though she knew about my rejection and had decided that a dose of potassium would somehow turn my day around. Choong Li was nowhere to be found and as much as I hoped that Mee Lan would open her mouth and tell me I knew that talking monkeys did not in fact exist and I walked around the house with the monkey trailing behind me. There were three rooms and the first one I entered was clearly Mee Lan's. A little lace-decorated cot stood, with crooked legs, near the door, bearing within it, a baby bolster wrapped in a soiled blanket. Hung on the walls were pictures of all kinds of monkey, the biggest one of a blank-faced *beruk*. A half-painted canvas screwed onto an easel leaned against the wall, anticipating a fall. It was not a very beautiful painting. Splashes of colour seemed to be its only definition.

The second room, I figured, was Choong Li's bedroom and it consisted of a bed, a cupboard and a nightstand. The walls were pictureless and decoration came in the form of dots of mould that seemed to be making a structured journey around the room. There was something innocently melancholic about everything here, from the few practical objects to the spontaneous decay that prevented the walls from being irredeemably plain.

I found Choong Li in the final room, lying on the floor, with her eyes closed, next to a large pot filled with burning incense and a jar of hibiscus flowers. Soft Chinese music was playing in the background, thick, eerie songs that reminded me of pagodas and dark rooms and the kind of grief that can only be found at funerals. At first I thought she was conducting a ritual in remembrance of her husband. But as I looked around the room I saw pictures of a white-faced, red-lipped woman dressed in elaborate, dramatic robes hung on the walls, leaving no space for the travelling ambitions of mould. And then I saw the shrine; medium-sized, orange and overflowing with more pictures of the woman, it outdid the melancholy of her bedroom perhaps because what was going on here was deliberate. I wanted to leave before Choong Li saw that I was there, looking on at her private moment as if it could be taken away by anybody who happened to pass by, as if it was that cheap and accessible. But without opening her eyes she said, 'Come, Kumar. I'm glad Mee Lan brought you here.' So the woman-monkey unit had conceived this trick. Well, it wasn't exactly a trick but I felt a little used like a tea towel that's been secretly borrowed to wipe spillage in the toilet.

'Sit with Auntie,' she said and I sat down in front of the shrine, keeping my silence because I knew that, like the last time, I wouldn't need to ask questions. In fact, I wouldn't even need to say anything. All Choong Li required was a pair of human ears to absorb her venom, sadness, regret.

'You know who that is in the pictures?' she asked, her eyes still closed. Her face had the look of peace that sinners possess when they have come to terms with their crime. Oh Rama, I thought, Oh Rama what has this woman done? Perhaps this was the woman she had murdered. Or maybe this was a long-dead sister who had been raped and killed.

I simply whispered out a no and she laughed, inappropriately I felt, since nothing funny had been said or done.

'It's Auntie lah,' she said trivially.

'I see,' I said, relieved, uncomfortable, unsure.

She opened her eyes and rose. She didn't say anything more. Instead she burst out into song. She had a shrill, falsetto voice and her face became plasticized, stretching and weaving itself into a vast array of expressions that was at once impressive and intimidating. I wasn't sure if I was expected to look surprised or excited, happy or sad, and so I looked around the room, nervous that she had finally submitted to the rumours regarding her mental health. I waited for her to finish what was obviously a necessity that had sprung quite suddenly from her soul. But after the first song she moved on to the next Chinese operatic number and I felt my organs sinking into one another. It wasn't that she wasn't hitting the notes because she was and no one could say that she didn't have a good voice for this kind of music. It was just that I wasn't a fan of Chinese opera and I was beginning to get irritated. When she started singing the third song, I got up and headed towards the door. It was only when I had nearly left that she stopped.

'Eh, Kumar,' she said, 'Auntie not yet finish. Where you going?'

'Home.'

'Wait. Wait. You don't want to know more?'

'Only if you stop singing.'

She looked a little hurt and I felt bad but the truth was that I would not have been able to sit through another song, and the way things were going, she would have carried on crooning without taking into account even the passing of days.

She agreed not to sing so long as I listened to her story, which pleased me since I really wanted to know all about what had made Mee Lan indispensable to her. So we sat in the room where pictures of her operatic self stared back at us with vengeance, then with pity, sadness, lust and anger. She gave me detailed stories of each picture, how and what she had performed years ago – against the wishes of her father who had educated her in private institutions and was determined for her to become a top-notch lawyer – when she had been a single, supposedly beautiful and talented opera singer who, she said with clear regret in her voice, was finally swept off the stage by one of her fans – the man who speedily morphed into her husband.

'And here's the twist of fate. Aiyah, really, Kumar, what a twist, you know. He was the one who followed me around the country, came to every opera, bought me flowers, chocolates, cards, everything lah. Then we got married. Ah ha. That was it lah. He couldn't take it. You know what he said?'

I really didn't appreciate those pauses she was fond of producing after throwing out a question that I could never answer. I thought perhaps a smile would do.

'That's right. He said, 'I cannot stand you standing on that stage like a common whore for all the men to have eye-sex with.' You ever heard of eye-sex, Kumar? That man was mad, I tell you. He was good at cooking, cleaning, watering plants and all that. But he refused, refused, just went on refusing to stay at home. Then one day he bought two bus tickets and moved us to this . . . this bloody *kampung* place. What to do? He went and bought that cinema with his father's money and banned me from singing. He gave me a new job. Ticket collector. You know what I did with that job? I went to the movies. Every day I watched and watched and watched.'

No tears had formed in her eyes but she might as well have been crying. Her voice had that tone that comes with lives that have been distorted by a single external force. I imagined her in the cinema, watching movie after movie in which she soon found herself getting lost and comfortable, creating another world, a performative one which reminded her of her past, a world that allowed for the revival of instincts that reality submerged for its own survival. Surely she would have grown into her favourite characters, none of whom her husband would have recognized because he seemed like the kind of man who could never have understood the need for a touch of spice in life, or people's capacity for creating alternatives for themselves. He had wanted a wife and a life in which he came out first and he made that happen every time he instructed his wife on her cinema duties and condemned her for her shoddy housekeeping. Choong Li's story made me think of Lady Chatterley or Madame Bovary although I couldn't see her as a sexual sort of person. Perhaps it was the frustration they had that I saw in her.

'Twenty years, you know, Kumar, he went on complaining about how I cooked rice. Then the floor was too dusty. Then the bed was not made. Aiyah. How to tell him that I was not born to dust cabinets? You know what it feels like to be on stage with hundreds of eyes watching you? Like a balloon, that's what. Only there, on that stage, I could understand things. You know what I mean? *Really* understand things. If I told him, I would get a nice slap on the face. Even if I didn't tell, a slap would come.'

Every day of her marriage must have been a slow but confirmed slaughtering of the self that had worn thick white face powder and dramatic eyebrows to find through the masks and the acting something truer than reality.

'If my husband didn't tell me for the thousandth time the night before he died, "Good for nothing, cannot even keep the house clean, where got wife like this?" you think Mee Lan would be here? Then, somehow, the next day was one very bright day. The sun, oh, the sun, it was shining like mad. It was like a God-day. Suddenly, I felt no, no, no, no more of this. A *beruk* was outside, climbing the coconut tree. And then I knew what to say. I said, "So you think I am not a woman since the house is not clean. Then if you are a man, you go and do something manly lah. Go and pluck coconuts with an ape. Or even better, see if you can *beat* the ape."'

I held my breath. What a *wild* thing to have done. I had to ask, 'Why a monkey?' and she looked at me as though I was the silliest person she had ever seen. I think I might have blushed a bit.

'Who can beat a *beruk* at coconut-plucking? That monkey saved me. It's . . . it's like a symbol, you know. *My* symbol. Any damn monkey is my symbol now. You see? Aiyah. I never even went to Mrs Mano. I told her ssshhh, don't say anything. Let me have my monkey. You can prove to people that you're a real psychic. She said okay. After all, Kumar, a monkey is the closest thing to being a person again, correct or not? Look at Mee Lan.'

At that moment, Mee Lan walked in with a plate of sliced watermelon, the red kind, and I looked at Choong Li sadly, realizing the extent of her pain, the reality of her convictions of non-belonging, what the disconnection from the thing she was meant to do in this life had done to her.

'Why don't you move from here and start singing again?' I asked, looking at the watermelon and wondering what I should do.

'No,' she said, chewing on the fruit, 'no, all I have now are memories and I need to make something new out of them. The past has taken me. That's why, Kumar, people should always do what they have to do.'

I braved the fruit. What harm could red watermelon do to the system, anyway? I closed my eyes and pushed my teeth into its red, spongy body. It was simply watermelon. A red watermelon and a yellow watermelon, I wanted to announce through a loudspeaker, are *watermelons*. Those sorts of things had to be written down, printed, bound, read about. And since no one else had done it, I would have to do it myself.

On my way back from Choong Li's house I saw Mrs Teng sitting in her garden, pretending to read the newspaper.

'Mrs Teng,' I shouted and she ran clumsily to her gate.

'Well, boy, what you find out?' she said, holding on to her asthma pump.

'There's a shrine dedicated to a famous Hong Kong actress in one room and the monkey has its own bed.'

She took a puff from the pump and removed a mobile phone from her pocket.

I cycled back and announced to my parents that I was going to become a writer. My mother started hiccupping and my father, after all these years, finally delivered that punch.

2

The Coming of Kingfishers

UP WE WENT, towards where God had preserved a space for *us*, a reward for basing our decisions on *Him*. Mrs Teng, who remained behind me until we reached the top, kept wheezing, 'Aisay, die lah like this,' as I heard bits of stone crumbling. 'Hush, hush,' I said when Nisha Siva grumbled as well, 'we haven't got our prize yet.' The girl, whose blouse buttons seemed to pop as we gained height, wasn't just holding on to the rock, she hugged it, unable, at times, to say goodbye to the current chunk and proceed to the next. Bringing the believers up made my feet loose, like they could detach themselves from my body whenever they wanted to.

But, in the end, my feet stayed faithful to my body. I looked up. There would be no more stones or rocks to hold on to as I dragged myself towards the heaven I had created. We had reached. 'Thanks God,' Mrs Teng screamed, 'Thanks God.' She threw her rucksack on the earth, creating a miasma of dust – the first dust, I thought – and she bent down, with grace I had never suspected she had, removing tins of sardines, baked beans, tuna and *sotong* she had clearly packed with a degree of love.

On a Thursday morning about a month ago the sky was a carpet of blue bird wings. This had happened only once before when the kingfishers arrived together, in one communal party, demonstrating their friendship but bringing with this fraternity, a big change in the weather. On other days they are alone, one perched on a tree branch, another high up on a lamppost as if they weren't the same kind of bird, as if their intentions were wholly different.

When the kingfisher flock came the last time, the island was almost destroyed. The sea pulled back, all the way to the peninsula, and for a few minutes we saw the bottom of the sea, dry and full of fumbling sea life. Then the sea came back, high and fast, eating everything it touched, not even stopping to burp. Seventy people died and I lost my home which my husband had built back in the '80s when we were first married. In the beginning it was just a simple single-storey house but over time, with the money we accumulated, it became bigger, better, a real testament to our value. When it was beaten by the sea, it took us years to rebuild it, but we did, and it was a much grander house. Beyond its Roman pillars and endless patio is the fact that I developed my special powers in this house, something which the business of ageing has taught me is a more beautiful thing than a set of Delft blue china.

On the day the house was completed I saw my first vision. It was a quick wild one, a simple flash of yellow light, jerking left to right with a clear enough face to indicate that it was Mulaika, the student who had drowned in the school toilet tub when I was headmistress. How was I to know that she would die a day after I said to her, 'Mulaika Abdul Rahman, you don't need to lie anymore. God punishes those who refuse to follow the laws of honesty. Admit to me now. Say "I stole the pink Manila card". The girl, daughter of government hospital nurses, said, "I . . . I . . . st . . . stole the pink . . . Manila card".' Where was the conviction? Of course I had to cane her. The next day, she was dead and the girl's mother appeared at my desk. 'Mrs Mano,' she said, sobbing, 'how you can do this to my daughter?'

'I did nothing,' I replied, 'the girl did the drowning all by herself.'

'Empty heart is what you got. You beating all the children here.'

How do you explain educational tactics to a government hospital nurse? She wouldn't have understood that I beat her daughter for the sake of her soul, to save her from fate, from the curse of her heritage.

My goodwill went unnoticed. Oh, of course I heard what those numbskulls said about me. 'Syaitan teacher,' they persisted, 'that Mrs Mano, balding, fattening Mrs Mano, she got evil black eyes, skin like bitter gourd, no children at home that barren bitch.' I never heard one person mention all those elements in a single sentence; the qualities, mine apparently, spread through many mouths, surfacing at town meetings, public dinners, the school staff room.

But I knew that what I was doing was right. When God *Himself* is telling you to save children from becoming like their parents, then you have to go all out, lecture, beat, coax, squeeze, slap, puncture, invigorate the soul again. I was simply performing a divine chore. What nobody knew was that on the day Mulaika died I locked myself in my prayer room and wept, not because of guilt or fear but because a girl had not been given a chance to redeem herself. I prayed for her soul and hoped that she understood the gravity of things now that she was dead and floating around the planet, watching the living suffer, fail and fool themselves. And then when Mulaika came to me I knew my prayers had been answered.

I woke up that Thursday morning, saw the birds flapping away, creating an unsettled sheet of blue life, and turned over to my husband. 'Baba,' I said, 'get ready'. He gave me that look which he gives me every time I mention a vision. His eyebrows begin a journey to meet each other while his cheeks rise slowly, slowly, towards the top of his face. When he does that I feel like I've flown to a cloud, and I'm about to step foot in it, to begin a long cosy sleep, only to discover that it's not an actual *thing*. He thinks I create these visions, that I am a fabricator of stories, a woman with a head full of hidden people and events that are waiting to be pieced together. 'Why don't you take up crocheting?' he told me after the third or fourth vision. When he said that, I could see spirits flying around my legs. At least I had them.

I looked at my believers, proud of them, grateful that there were still people on the island who refused to yield to cynicism. I said, 'Dear friends, thank you so much for having faith in my gift. Fifteen people out of thousands? We are the select few who have managed to listen to God's voice. The rest, sad to say, need time to discover their inner divinity. And when the disaster hits, only then will they realize that all they needed was just a little bit of faith. But that is for them to learn. Tonight we'll get to know each other. We should also pray together, pray for our loved ones who refused to believe.' They clapped for me, nodding, tearful too, and Jessie Foong, the main disseminator of my visions, shouted, 'Yes, woo hoo, yes.'

'Tell us, Mrs Mano, just how to get this prediction,' Rafidah Rosli said, the most unlikely person to be on this hilltop. Three years ago, her son received five fine pinches from me for talking in class. After that, Rafidah wiped me out as a human being altogether. How did she do that? She simply refused to believe that I existed. Once, at the market, we stood next to each other, buying fish, and the fishmonger said, 'Sorry lah, Auntie, but the lady beside you already bought the last *ikan merah*.' Rafidah replied, 'There's no lady beside me. What lie are you telling?' Faith has the power to bring people back to life. Her son, also brought along to witness that force, stared at me.

'It was the kingfishers. They came again in a flock, just like they did when the last tsunami hit us. This morning I saw them outside my window and I knew that something bad was going to happen. I had to warn people. I had to save the island.'

'Such a noble woman,' Jessie Foong said and I was applauded once again.

'You all also would do the same if you had my gift, I'm sure. Now that we are here together, united by our passion for life, we should find a way to connect with one another. What do you think?'

Nisha Siva said, 'Yes, Auntie. We should all share something. Something deep and personal. A secret.'

Silence. Were we really ready for secrets? We had no choice now. We had already mounted the hill.

'Okay, let me see,' I said, 'this is not really a secret. More of a confession of my feelings. Some of you still think that I was a witch at school but the proper truth is that I was thinking, every time I hit or pinched or punished, of the souls of those children. They had to know the meaning of evil and of good. So of course parents hated me, they still do I know, but the kids needed to be saved from becoming like their elders.'

The light of the afternoon sun illuminated the faces in front of me so that they looked like a crowd of bright, unreal creatures who had congregated to listen to the enlightened, to the spark of God that had descended to earthly shores (pardon the insensitive analogy) to bless and teach, serve and inspire victims of their own conditions. In that instance, as the faces shone and looked back at me with yearning and suffering, the memory of the kingfishers appeared. This was my moment of divine service. I had to share the truth of this world with them which they, the chosen fourteen, were in need of hearing after years of fraudulence, grief, sickness and confusion. So I told them as the sun made the moment singular, incandescent, pure, 'My visions came because God wanted everyone to know that this life, people, this life we have is not the *only* life. You understand? The pain is not real, no, my children, not real at all. Once in a while God wants Himself to be heard. That's why I have these visions, these little clues that He drops to tell us, "I ALSO LIVE."'

My mouth felt like I had eaten a dry biscuit. I waited for the claps but they didn't manifest. The believers watched me with round, enlarged eyes, sitting in silence which seemed to be a necessary precursor for their thousand questions and comments that came like a cacophony, like the squawks of frightened birds. Why do you talk like a prophet? You think you are so special. How do you know if they are actually visions? You sound like you think you're God. How can this gift suddenly appear? Maybe what you have is a big imagination. Why should we believe you?

The challenge was absurd, especially after the sun had brought about the believers' momentary transformation into passive spectres. I knew that prophets and spiritual beings of the past had to encounter all kinds of contestation. Jesus Christ had to be stoned and crucified. He had to perform the miracle of resurrection to prove his identity. Of course I wouldn't be stoned or crucified – the fourteen people in front of me were not the killing kind, I was sure – but I had my own miracle to show. 'Please, please, believers, just wait and see. Patience. You know what that is? Ah, yes. Be patient. Tomorrow you will see, as we descend this hill, a wet world. Now what do we do? We keep the faith. We trust. If you can trust, then you can conquer the world. Let me show you how. Be free with your secrets. And *trust* that the believers will keep them.'

'What better way?' Jessie Foong said, smiling as though she had realized something monumental. 'It's true lah. Why did we come here in the first place? For faith, like Mrs Mano says. We are the only people who really believe in trust. Come lah, let's be brave.'

They looked at each other. Then the mouths, slowly, willingly, disgorged the depths of their lives.

Choong Li had been a Chinese opera singer. Rafidah cried when she found out that she was pregnant with her second child. Nisha was a depressive. Jessie Foong had severed ties with her only sister. Tamarind Cheah locked herself in a room and prayed every time it rained. Kumar Balan's father had stopped speaking to him ever since he announced that he was a writer. Josie D'Cruz wished that she was white. Vani Muthu put plastic in her curry puffs to make them crunchier and her customers more satisfied. Sarimah Abu Bakar wanted to leave her husband. Mrs Teng had a heart that could collapse at any time. Kavitha Thamboo had once aborted a child because she found out that her husband was having an affair. Chitra Lee slept one night a week. Vellu Krishnan regretted that he never married but only because he had to do his own housekeeping. Carol Lim enjoyed abusing cats.

A few people in the neighbourhood were immediate believers in my gift. Vani Muthu, my first customer, rushed to see me when she found out. 'A few weeks ago,' she said, 'my wonderful, beautiful, lovely darling Rajamuthu was taken away from me. Can you contact him please?'

'I will need something personal of his first. Anything. A T-shirt, a watch, whatever.'

She brought out a plastic toy dish. 'Here, Rajamuthu *loved* to drink out of this.'

'Just what kind of a person was this Rajamuthu?'

'Not a person lah, Mrs Mano. He was my beautiful, wonderful, darling hamster.'

'I'm sorry,' I had to say, 'I don't do hamsters.' She turned away, weeping.

'But,' I continued, 'do you have a dead *person* to contact?' She did, a cousin twice removed, and I couldn't have asked for better news.

After Vani Muthu, a few more believers trickled in. Of course, some came just to be sensationalized so that they would have something to tell their neighbours. 'That Mrs Mano ah,' I heard Jessie Foong say to Kumar Balan, 'saw Tamarind's father's father and he told her heaven is full of Africans. That woman has real power. I tell you, Kumar, power these days, can get anywhere lah.' But many also sided with my husband, insisting that I was creating these visions out of my talent for invention and my sick desire for trickery.

The last time the kingfishers came no one noticed them. 'Baba,' I told my husband after our house had been destroyed, 'it was the kingfishers, you know. They came to warn us that the sea was going to attack Coal Island. We just ignored them only.'

The look didn't take long to form on his face. He replied, 'Pyrex glasses, downstairs hall and upstairs hall furniture, kitchen sink, bathroom sink, ceramic tiles. Must get Ah Kong to bring the van tomorrow so we can fit everything in.'

I told a few other people, one or two nodded while the rest laughed and laughed. But that Thursday morning, when I saw the bright blue wings, I decided that I would save the island. People who thought I was either a cruel teacher or a fake mystic would finally have to accept my compassion and divine power.

I went to my computer and created a flyer that read in bold blue letters 'TSUNAMI TO HIT COAL ISLAND TODAY. PREPARE TO EVACUATE.' I printed one copy and headed to the photocopying shop, feeling a little displaced because I had not stepped into Chester Wong's shop since I made his daughter admit in front of the school assembly that she had cheated in the end of term exam. That afternoon he arrived at my office and said, 'So you go and strike again. How many children you want to break, hah? You wait and see. If you carry on this nonsense, I know someone in the ministry. Big man. I'll get you out of here once and for all.' I didn't reply. Education should be left to educators, I wanted to say, but he would not have listened. When news of my special powers first became public, he told Kumar Balan, one of his regular customers, 'You see what that rat is doing? Pah! Now suddenly she is one big holy lady. She wants us to say, 'We forgive you,' by pretending that God, dunno what God lah, picked her to talk to ghosts.' I glided out from behind the notebook shelf and waved my sari against his face which had lost its critical hue once the realization that I had been eavesdropping hit him.

But I wasn't going to let the past interfere with the fate of the island. I walked in, my shoulders firm, my spine erect, noticing the widening of his eyes when I said, 'One thousand copies please.' He scanned the paper, shook his head and said in a clear, fierce voice, 'No'. I stared at him and softened my face. 'Please, Chester. We must forgive and forget. The past is over,' I said.

'I know how to forgive and forget. That's why I'm not allowing you to make a fool of yourself. I know what you're doing, Mrs Mano, and I can't help you.'

'I am trying to save the island.'

'No, you're trying to save your reputation.'

'Please, Chester. This has nothing to do with me. This is about the rest of the island. A Tsunami is coming and we have to leave.'

'Oh so now you've become a prophet. Not just a ghost detector. God must be on our side since he's blessed us with your presence.'

'Just print the copies and start packing up.'

But Chester Wong sat down and sipped his morning tea. To save an island you have to be bold and think like a survivalist. I picked up a chair, hit Chester on his head, made one thousand copies of the flyer and started delivering them to shops and houses, knowing that even if I didn't manage to cover everyone, word would spread soon enough and we'd escape the sea's revenge.

But oh! The disbelievers! 'What nonsense you spreading here, ah Mano's wife?' Mr Chong shouted, tearing up the flyer into enough pieces to make a dazzling display of confetti. Even Uncle Nizam, ninety years old and sedate, told me, flailing his walking stick in the air, 'Crazy people like you should leave. Only then we'll be free of disaster on the island.' I suppose they felt as if God was abusing them, that the earth was acting like a rebellious child and we, the innocent, hardworking citizens were having to rearrange our lives without a chance of opposing this inevitability.

But the believers assembled around me. Choong Li, the monkey-lady, said, 'Aiyah. This is too bad. Just when you thought life had gone back to normal. Then this thing comes. You know, without my Mee Lan, I would just stay in the house and do nothing. Let the stupid sea come and take me. But now . . . with my monkey . . . it's different lah.' Kavitha Thamboo agreed. 'Of course, of course. We must spread the word.'

Two hours later word had indeed spread. But the word, originally fresh and real in Kavitha's mouth, got tweaked in somebody else's. Mrs Mano, it seemed, the spiteful educator and quack visionary, had created a cult for the vulnerable and the gullible and she was sabotaging the peace of the island by duping people into leaving through an unkind prediction of their imminent deaths. That's the island for you. It compels you to welcome bruises to the heart, to even play around with the nips and stings but in the end, if you want to carry on as God had intended, you forget the pain, forget that you had once been its keeper.

When I returned home to pack my survival kit, I found my husband sitting in the hall, staring at a wall, firming up his fists, making crik crik noises with his teeth like a man who has decided that for a moment, he would like to try out, for nostalgic purposes, what it would feel like to be a provoked schoolboy during recess time. 'Oi,' he said in the deep voice that he used whenever he was trying to get me to listen to him seriously, 'now fully gone mad lah, I suppose? Sit here and don't move. I won't have people wondering what sort of woman I married. Let the Tsunami come. Maybe then only you'll learn to shut up your mouth and act properly.' In the past when he had thrown out orders, I obeyed quietly especially when I saw him removing his belt. But now, in the face of a roly-poly tragedy, I had to bypass the belt and save what actually mattered in life: life itself. I told him, 'Baba, I'm telling the truth. I saw this morning. The birds came like the last time and look what happened then? We lost our house. We were lucky then not to have died. We might not be so lucky again. Come, Baba, come and help me pack.'

He removed his belt and I ran to the bedroom, locked myself in, packed my valuables and left through the window. A group of people waited for me down the road – the believers – and we began our journey towards the hill as advised by Nisha Siva who said that we should be well above sea level in order to avoid getting hit by the treacherous waves of the sea. Fifteen of us got into Mrs D'Cruz's van and we rode fifteen miles out to the foot of the highest hill on Coal Island. 'Okay,' I said when we arrived, 'now we all have to climb this, understand? The weaker ones, you make sure you're next to the strong ones. The strong ones, make sure you look out for the weaker ones. People, let's save ourselves.'

Night materialized, suddenly. Against our expectations, sleep was not its shadow, rather a distant dream, forever beyond this world. Confessions, too precious to be heard closer to sea level, lined up in my head, and certainly too, in theirs. One by one, the confessions bowed and spoke. Mosquitoes moved in sync with those secrets, dipping towards the ear during the transition of voices. On and on, as the sky darkened, presenting dots of light, and then as it paled, the sun's head pushing past the rubber estates, noises persisted within, against the deep, terrifying silence of the hilltop, the mosquitoes the best examples of that condition, being unnoticed until they nearly made their way into earlobes.

'Come, come, morning already,' Tamarind Cheah said, 'better we go now. Tsunami sure finish.'

The descent was quicker, less wordy than the ascent. There was no mention of the night before. The sighting of Mrs D'Cruz's metallic purple van was one of those privately joyous moments. Then it got harder. The sun was bright, superior to the previous days and beauty dwelt even in the silliest of spots, like in the drains, speckled, so it seemed, with pearls. The sun could do that sometimes. The engine droned on, the only thing that made our ears work. Then the facts of the scenery, to which our eyes had been prone, sitting in the van as we were with nothing else to do, compelled Rafidah Rosli to say, 'Somewhere in my heart I thought I knew. What stupid tsunami?'

Mrs D'Cruz dropped me off first and when it was time for me to turn away, a goodbye of sorts, she said, 'Okay then. I guess that's about as much as we can handle for now.' The rest stayed faithful to their seats, observing the scenery.

I walked into my home and found my husband gone. It wasn't simply that he had left for work. His possessions were missing but more than that, I could smell his absence. And then I found his note which read, 'Ambigai, the divorce papers will be arriving any day now. All the best, Mano.'

He had gone. Really?

That man? Gone?

Whatever for?

I waited for him, afraid to leave the house in case he came back. But weeks escaped in my solitude. And no one came, not a single believer. They had felt cheated, I suppose. But the kingfishers, they really did flock in blue.

Then a miracle happened. Kavitha Thamboo's husband died of a heart attack in a mysterious location and she knocked on my door, pleading that I ask his spirit for answers. I welcomed her and said, 'Now you believe?' She smiled and replied, 'I don't think any of us really stopped believing. Some things like faith are just necessary. Otherwise, what do we have? And if any of them doubt you, they'll never say anything, not after our day on the hill.'

That night I dreamt of kingfishers. Thousands swirled in

the sky and my husband appeared with blue wings, slowly changing into a kingfisher and when he had become a full bird he said, 'It's the small things that are big. You should use your heart more.' So he approved of my gift, after all. He left only so that I could carry on receiving my visions without domestic encumbrances. What did it matter that the tsunami had never come? The real point was that the kingfishers had.

The next day I received a note from him which read, 'You are a silly witch who has no heart. You will pay for your stupid visions, believe me, woman, one of these days you will pay for all the damage.'

The dream and the note. Don't dreams give truths that are truer than the truth? Of course. Deep in his soul he believed in my gifts and wanted them to be real. He just didn't know it yet.

Since then I have not seen kingfishers again, whether in the sky or in my dreams. Left with ghosts of the dead who still have a passion for the living, I work out the world with them. 'The eyes, keep them open, and in the wildness that you see, there is power and order,' they tell me. Soon, I am quite sure, I will be meeting God himself. When that happens, no one on Coal Island will dare to say that all I am is a devouring teacher and a sham spiritualist. Instead they will hold me up in the air and say that I am God's next-door neighbour and nobody can beat that title. I will, like the prophets before me, finally be proving my power.

3

The Python's Meal

VALLI HAS LEFT me. This life is a brewery.

Short, immediate observations – active realizations – come and go, never going, always coming. The path to intoxication has to be brewed for it does not naturally build itself and it has to be brewed in secret for it must appear fluid, effortless. In reality, the giddiness has been there from birth and it inches towards the rest of age and the affair is a violent dream. After the battles, parties, kissing and beating, each life returns to its individual maxims.

Valli has left me. This life is a brewery.

And then there is the wildness, indeed, the utter wildness of the other world, the one that is forever apart from what is known. The untamed that cannot be tamed.

How can glory and guilt exist simultaneously? Yet, they do. One has to be suppressed, waiting patiently.

Eighty years ago, when I was a young man with a passion

for escapades, ships and salty air, I left a dark Victorian house in the Midlands and began my life on Coal Island in Malaya, then under British rule and prospering in the production of coal, rubber and coffee. My youth had been a banal affair. Mother, apron-clad, swooped into rooms carrying silver trays that wobbled with the weight of crumpets, toast and large pots of tea. 'The teapot has the potential to master the world,' she'd say, sipping on tea with her eyes closed, purring, considering my father, I always thought, who was away somewhere in Africa or India. A man of the empire, he went off to sleep next to white tigers and zebras, waking up to jewelled palaces and big mimosa trees, not to scenes of brick buildings blurred by thick fog and the soot of industry. Blackberry jam, yes, Mother loved blackberry jam as well.

Theodore and Felix, my brothers, were rarely a part of those observations. I don't think they cared much that Mother loved tasting tea so that she could land in the tropics where Father was conquering beasts. They simply played together, always. No direct disapproval of me had been issued but in each other's company, they were whole, and it was obvious that additional elements to their joint time were regarded by them to be superfluous and therefore frivolous. 'How charming Percy looks today with his little starched bowtie,' Felix once laughed as we prepared for Sunday Church. With a mother susceptible to tannin-adventures and brothers who would have been better off being born as one person, the house was still. I would sit on a stool by the furnace, and with the flames charging at each other in front of my eyes, I dived in, not literally of course. It was the heat I took away, the heat of Father's Eastern World.

When I became a teenager and threatened to follow in my father's footsteps, my mother would weep, not gently or with feminine fragility, but violently as though she were in childbirth or was having a limb taken off. It bothered me that she had no grace when she tried to deter me from my adventures, and it was precisely because she was vulgar in her emotions that I had to disassociate myself from an atmosphere where mothers sought to trap their sons with turbulent love and personal inadequacy. Of course she would never understand the urgency of upholding the empire because that required a solid mind and a heart that found fulfilment in important things like aiding the uncivilized towards shedding their savagery, or in my personal opinion, maintaining it. Fighting my mother off seemed impossible until news of my father's death arrived and she surrendered her strength, day-by-day growing further into a stone-eyed daze and I, knowing that my siblings would do nothing, checked her into an asylum where she was diagnosed with severe melancholia. Finally, I was free to leave the damp and the tea-talk, the damp tea-talk. I was ready to give myself to the tropics.

A few months later, at the age of seventeen, I headed for Malaya where I was to work as a clerk for the manager of a rubber plantation on an island I had never heard of before. I remember looking out to sea, watching the dark purple waves turn and clash, thinking, 'Here I am. Just like Raffles.'

I arrived in Malaya, ambition thick in my lungs, feeling

the flaming air froth up my blood, those Coventry furnace flames having followed me across the ocean. It is impossible to trace how that heat built a home in my body, how it drummed in lavish rhythms through the tepid winds and urged me to say to myself on nights when the moon seemed to invest in my soul, 'More, all the while, more. You have the spark that so many depend on.' And for years I clutched on to those words, went around with them, lived on them. But such words shatter and when they do, you are forever bound to solitude. Acts of compassion do not bring those words back. Valli made sure they did not resurrect. They did, however, figure as ghosts.

'Child, what is the matter?' I had said to her ten years ago.

A girl, filly-eyed, sat against a coconut tree, watching the sky as though she had made a career out of it.

'It might not be too safe to be sitting here all by yourself. Where are your parents?' I carried on in Tamil, sensing that, perhaps, she was not fluent in English.

She turned to look at me. 'But you're a vellaikaran'. A tear dripped onto the sand, making a momentary mark before getting absorbed.

'Yes. A good observation, indeed. You're rather bright. Still, are you alone?'

She nodded, letting the tears flow without impediment. 'My Appa and Amma gave their lives to a motorcycle. Appa just got it, you know. They went to buy me a new bag for school. I never got it.'

Each word manifested a face and the faces grew, numerically, colliding into one another so that they were, contradictorily, both my coolie women and my bastard children, flashing their dark eyes at me, cursing, accusing, coal-skinned and pitiful. When the faces separated, the mothers were thanking me in my bed, bending their heads as they accepted a jar of raspberry jam or a box of expired chocolates shipped all the way from England.

'I'm sorry, child, I'm truly very sorry,' I said, trying to blink out the faces but they soared like swallows, bursting and regenerating, bursting and regenerating. 'Is there anyone who wants you?'

'There is nobody here but me.'

How was it that I had never seen such a plain dark face before? The eyes and lips, still being worked out for maturity, invited me elsewhere, well outside of time and beyond the plantation. In the end, the thing that governs us occasionally supplies a portal or two for collapsing the past and the present. Recognizing the portal remains the challenge. And how the past can reform itself when portal and revelation meet!

'Then you will live with me. I will teach you everything,' I said, finding my own willingness a revelation.

She came with me, in shock, trembling I suppose, because her life was changing.

Days passed well. She joined me in the kitchen, cooking curries and boiling rice, cleaning pans, scrubbing at serving spoons thick with the memory of spices. We read together, her affinity for absorbing poetry and the classics a miraculous thing to witness. Even more stupendous was her endless desire to know *everything*. 'I want to know *alllll* your stories,' she said to me, a mere few weeks after she had moved in.

Honesty is a tricky phenomenon. Yes, phenomenon. It unravels just as it does the unravelling. But at that point, when she had wanted 'alllll' my stories, having taken her in, honesty became redundant.

A father cannot say to his daughter, 'My coolie women's husbands were skilled at pretending that their wives came to my home to polish my brass lamps or to dust my cabinets. It was how they could survive and enjoy the imported goods that their wives brought back but when the babies popped out with buttery skin, certain husbands worked badly on the plantation. They arrived late and made slipshod incisions on the trees so that we were not producing as much rubber as we had to. I fired those men who were bold enough to exercise their revenge, knowing that there were always coolies to be had, an endless line of desperate men who would sacrifice their wives for a few cents and a loaf of white bread.' That is honesty, blank-faced, stakeless honesty. A father can't do that to his child.

How do you say, 'This is fresh. Why awaken dust? I want to be new again with you?' The more I fostered hope that our relationship could stand without crutches from the past, the more her need for explanations deepened.

Honesty skirted the perimeters of our words, our movements, its impossibility compelling me to turn to paper where I composed digested ruminations about my life that Valli longed to understand but would never see.

I carried on enjoying my life on the plantation, with little to stop me except for brief instances of guilt when a few of my women drank weed killer as a result of their discovery that they could never have a life beyond the plantation and that their only route to another world was through me, a blond-haired man who could tell them about snow and daffodils and Christmas. But after a while even those tales and my gifts of soap and lotion and confectionary could not appease their burgeoning lust for death. I noticed that the women who gave in to a non-material life were those who were happy wives and discontented mistresses. They were the ones who never allowed me to scan the depths of their eyes or to spread my tongue on their lips. They entered my bed with their heads hung low and their bodies stiff with self-loathing, smelling of coconut oil, knowing as they carefully flung a well-moistened arm in my face, that I was repelled by their coolie scent which reminded me of disintegrating fruit. It was then that I held them tightly in my arms and refused to let them go. I liked to hear them scream because they could do nothing about the fact that my strength was too great even for their imaginations. When they left my bed, whimpering, sobbing, wrapping their saris with guilt around their throbbing bodies, I would light a cigar and dream about the people I knew back home who were sitting by fires, drinking brandy to soothe their icy bodies, unaware of the glory of the tropics, its complete difference from the insipid flatness of the temperate world. I was proud of my life on the rubber estate, proud of the coolie women I had conquered and my position as manager of hundreds of men and women who were too poor to contemplate a better life. My father would have done the same.

But my Valli persisted, intuitively feeling out my past, yearning for explanations, like any child.

'Father, why do people on this island hate us?' she asked me when she was fifteen. She had been down to the market and the fishmonger, a petty, impudent woman, told her that the fish she sold was reserved for decent human beings, not for sinners who lived for their perversions. I rarely went to the market, but on that particular day, the fisherman who usually brought me his best catches had taken ill. I sent Valli, thinking that people would treat an innocent coolie girl better than an old white man whose reputation was irreparable.

'Don't you know what small islands can breed? Filthy lies. You have done nothing wrong,' I said.

'Yes, but why won't you tell me *anything* about the olden days? You said you came from England to work here. But I want to know *more*, Father, *please*. Even if it's just *one* story. For instance, weren't you ever in love?'

Love, indeed. The most improbable kind of love, I wanted to say.

'Well, yes, a long time ago,' I replied, feeling too weak to resist her questions. They had been coming for years and would keep coming. At some point, I philosophized, my past (or at least its elements) and my future would have to meet.

'In England?'

'Oh no. England could not carry that kind of love.'

'Then what was England like?'

The poor child. She had never been beyond the island, beyond the house I had chosen for her.

'My days in England . . . ah yes, there, then, I was warrior, pirate, king, hero, lord of savage lands.'

She laughed. 'You mean like how?'

'Like in my lonely little mind. But enough of England. That's the way life was at that time.'

'Okay, okay, so,' she insisted, 'when you came here, what did you do? How was it different?'

'Oh, when I came, it was obvious. This new world, this old savage world had not been spoiled by the smooth gaze of machinery. Do you understand?'

She nodded. 'You always say that a rough patch of jungle is better than a television scene.'

'And right you are. The men and women who worked on the plantation, your people, migrants from India, their eyes like the eyes of a doe, oh they were quite fine specimens. The nose-rings the women wore . . . I had never seen anything like it. The wild-patterned fabric they wrapped themselves in . . . again, never in my life . . . the way they squatted when they ate their lunch, licked their fingers and fished into their meals with soggy, busy hands.'

'These were all my people, Father?'

'Yes, your people from India. I watched them from my office, amazed that they were even human, because they were, you know, so different from the people *I* knew. In England, we cut our meat with a knife and dabbed our lips with a napkin. And if you really liked a meal, you said, "Thank you". You didn't belch or smack your lips.'

'You liked them then?'

A juvenile mind could hardly grasp the complexities of

liking. How could I have said that I liked them but not in the way that Mother liked blackberry jam?

'That's one way of putting it,' I said, 'but at first, I didn't even know how to communicate with them. I rarely spoke when I began work as Mr Archibald Rutherford's clerk. I worked hard. Oh, how hard I worked! I typed letters, prepared documents. But I never went out to the plantations. I could hear the coolies coming, though, from my office. Their anklets rang like tiny church bells. They'd walk right past my window, their bodies poised, elegant, ready for toiling. The first few years, all I did was observe them. Sometimes I'd write to my mother, telling her about my strange new life. It was a shame, I thought, to have come all the way to the East and say nothing to the *real* folk here.'

'So what did you do?'

She was teasing the Honesty Phenomenon once again. But it could only disentangle introspectively, on paper which I turned to immediately once Valli was tired out.

> I continued to watch. I fantasized about what it would be like to dress in those strange clothes and to eat with greed, hunger and simplicity from glimmering tiffin carriers, beneath trees, so confident in the knowledge that the natural world would always provide for them. The women seemed unaware of the way their breasts swayed when they bent down to slash a rubber tree or of the plumpness of their hips when they knelt on the grass to serve their men food. I noticed how their faces were burnt and chiselled and their mouths were wide and deep as if they could consume whole globes and think nothing

> of it. The women came to me, oh yes, they came and said nothing. It was the easiest thing in the world. Yet, Mother's words, 'Always be suspicious when life becomes too easy, too available for you,' haunted me. But what did Mother know? She could only dream of Father. She never understood what he did in Africa, in India.

I said to Valli, 'I didn't do very much except work hard, to be honest. But I was learning Tamil. I wanted, so very badly, to speak to them. I also spent time working and studying. Like Raffles before me, you know Sir Stamford Raffles, I started examining the natural world and began collecting specimens to preserve and dissect. My house was soon filled with butterflies and spiders, tropical birds and snakes, colossal leaves, rare flowers. And then something big happened. On a rainy morning, before the sun had risen, Mr Rutherford was found by a group of tappers on their way to work. He lay decapitated under a row of rubber trees, his head placed politely on his chest. He was always nice to *us*. To the coolies, well, he simply didn't understand them. All my hard work paid off. I was given the plantation to manage.'

'Well done, Father! *Then* did you get to talk to the coolies and find out more about them?'

'Inevitably, yes.'

'Since you had liked them from the very start, you wouldn't have been like Mr Rutherford.'

'Yes'.

'And then what happened when you became manager?'

'I didn't abuse my coolies as Mr Rutherford had done. Oh

no, I didn't. My men and women would receive rewards for good work and breaks when necessary. I asked about their lives, made sure they had shoes . . . but enough of this.' Why couldn't Valli just accept that her presence was enough for me? And that I was enough for her?

'No, wait. You haven't finished yet. What about the woman you fell in love with?'

Yes, *her*. The coolie women all looked very similar to me but Sita Devi emerged out of them like a nugget of coal, glistening from early morning rain. My child would persist, if not today, then some other day, in knowing about the love that had once consumed me. An old man has little strength to fight off desires that come from the young.

'Well . . . what's there to say? Let me see . . . her eyes were large and black and when she walked she only looked ahead. She was a coolie on my plantation and, oh, how she did her work! Pragmatic, she was. She never really talked to anyone except during mealtimes when she offered to serve food. I suppose I was falling in love with her without knowing it. I soon found myself following her, discreetly, of course. She always had other women around her. But one evening as I was preparing to leave the office after a long day, I saw her walking alone.'

'Oh, Father,' my Valli interrupted, 'what did you do?'

'Well, I followed her of course . . . all the way to the temple. I hid behind a pillar, watching her pray. She performed the most curious rituals with bells and fire and milk. Then she sat on the temple steps, her eyes closed. There was a string of jasmine flowers in her hair . . .'

It was impossible not to return to her in my mind, remembering how my gut growled when I thought of smelling her, layered with all the strange scents of the temple, how I thought about the white-arched church from home and looked at the painted gods before me, recalling my only friend Tom, the hymn-singer, the psalm-memorizer, who would never have believed in God there since Jesus was a sedate, sad man with a few harmless streams of blood flowing gently down his arms and legs. That was what belonged in a house of God: something simple and tragic to remind us of the pain that would be our battle till the very end. But there – in that circus of a hundred gods – that effortless message was lost in abundant pluralities: multiple eyes, arms, legs. Colours seemed to grow in and out of each other. A blue-bodied man leapt out from a wall with what looked like a garden fork in his hand. Black babies were stepped on by a Hindu Medusa who stuck out a giant red tongue. A chunky elephant man in scarlet bloomers sat in a booth decorated with coconuts and lamps.

'Yes, and so, Father, what next?' Valli brought me back to her.

'Sorry. I was remembering something. Anyway, the coolie woman seemed to know exactly what she wanted from her gods. She dealt with each one differently, her face solemn, earnest. She was certain, I suppose, of her salvation. I had no choice, child, I had to worship her. The gods were useless to me. But she, with her constant attention to her statues, convinced me that she was beyond the plantation and the other coolies. It didn't matter to her if a white man abused her. If he did, she would just think of each god and whisper mantras into the air, transforming her tormentor into a believer.'

'Did you go and speak to her?' Valli asked.

'Oh no! She was too sacred for that. I merely watched her although I knew I'd have to talk to her one day, to save my heart, you know.'

I would follow her, Valli, like a man pursuing a ghost, knowing that he can never catch it. For the next few nights I would return to the temple, scanning her gait, looking for clues that would reveal her soul to me, my desire for her becoming more uncomfortable with every moment that I spent wondering what it would feel like to unravel her sari and take her in front of one of her gods.

'But I could never violate her. So you know what I did?' I continued.

Valli shook her head, eager, I imagined, for some kind of pinnacle to the story.

'I stopped following her to the temple.'

'But that's the craziest thing to do! Especially since you *loved* her and she didn't *know* it.'

'Well, what is life if not complex? Sita Devi was already married, you see, to another coolie called Muthiah. What was I to do?'

Valli's face stopped moving. Then she forcefully brought her head towards her open palms, letting it rest there until she had recovered enough to say, 'So you did the gentlemanly thing, huh, Father? A real Englishman you are.'

I didn't know what to say. To a certain extent, there had

always been great apertures between Sita Devi and I which would have qualified me to be the real Englishman that Valli seemed convinced I was.

But I couldn't confess to Valli that I longed for my dark pious coolie woman and made it my plan to catch her. She worked very quietly, like a shadow that moves about clandestinely, hoping never to be found out. But I was God of the plantation, an omniscient eye, watching her, wondering how I would word my offer of work. It was clear that Sita Devi and Muthiah were in love, for during lunch they were seen feeding each other, every ball of food placed with love into a seductively open mouth. But they were poor and needed my help.

'Well, I just had to be close to her, Valli, so I asked her if she wanted to earn extra money cleaning my house.'

'That was kind of you, Father. At least she got to take home some money while you healed your heart.'

Valli's words slammed into my ears, crippling my blood-flow.

Sita Devi's face returned to me, nodding slowly, sadly. There she was again arriving at my home, knowing that dust-cloths and brooms were not going to be her tools. I took her to the bedroom, untied her sari, and made love to her while her eyes remained fixed on the nocturnal trees outside the window, her hands positioned only once on my back, refusing to find rhythm and freedom. Bringing her back to life, in that moment, for Valli, reminded me of the body heat I had felt gathering in my heart, clumping up against the coldness that was left to my limbs. Every session was the same. Her eyes were *always* beyond me. Still, I insisted on her return, thinking I suppose, that one day I would appropriate her affection for Muthiah. Every visit made me feel lonelier. She had grown accustomed to averting my gaze and shielding herself from me even as I sucked on her flesh and nibbled on her black, deftly carved nose. The more distant she grew from me, the more coolies I conquered in my bed, a little more violently each time. Husbands were getting dissatisfied and I began to worry that I would end up like Mr Rutherford, my head on my heart. Matters got worse when the women started having my children and I was losing my grip on the men. They stopped listening to me and arrived at work drunk, violating my authority just as I had violated their domestic power. But I still didn't have Sita Devi and I was sinking into melancholy, staying true to my genes. I started writing to my mother more often but refrained from mentioning what my life had become.

'But you see, Valli, it didn't actually get easier, having her in my home. When you're older, you'll understand what it feels like to have love to give but no takers. And when that happens . . . you turn desperate. But remember not to act on that desperation. You could regret it forever.'

'I'm not sure I understand,' she said, squinting, 'but what I *really* want to know is what happened to Sita Devi.'

'Well, so it goes that one day a coolie called Ganesh came rushing into my office. 'Mista, Mista,' he screamed, 'got a python in the estate.' Being Hindus, they refused to confront snakes, no matter how threatening they were. A cobra on the plantation was once disposed of with a stick and a prayer.

But pythons were different. If you ask me, they look like specimens that have lingered on after the Jurassic era, and that's a very, very long time ago, child, when most animals were large, chunky things. Once, a python had been found on a neighbouring plantation coiled around a rubber tree with a whole goat in its stomach. So of course when Ganesh told me the news, I was somewhat afraid. But I had to do something. It was *my* plantation. I told myself I would try my best not to kill the beast since the Hindus would not be happy if I did. After the morning's tapping had been done and the coolies were in the rubber factory I packed my rifle and a newly sharpened butcher's knife, just in case, and entered the plantation as stealthily as I could. My eyes were alert to everything, just about everything brown and thick, and once or twice I imagined that I saw it sitting smugly underneath a tree but it had only been a fallen bark. It was dark and quiet in the plantation and the trees, weeping out their white blood, all of a sudden made me feel unreal, as though I had been placed in the staging of a peculiar play where the props were alive and extraordinary. This sensation which I thought would be fleeting remained whole and it made me blink more times than I normally did. I even pinched my arms to check my status. Was I alive or dead? I looked around, paranoid, panicked, thinking that the beast was watching me and devising its strategy to wrap itself around my body and take me into its mouth to quell the rumbles in its tummy. I heard the crunching of dead leaves. I held onto my rifle, prepared, if necessary, to show the creature why man ruled over the animal kingdom. I turned around and saw a coolie standing idly by a row of trees. He just stood there as though he were a free man whose time was his own. I was getting annoyed and I was about to say something when I saw it, making its way towards the coolie. I held on to my rifle and fired. Within seconds the beast was dead. The coolie came running towards me, panting, screaming, thankful. I recognized the face. It was Sita Devi's husband.'

'Father you are a hero,' Valli said, excited, awe filling her open mouth, 'You saved a man's life. But what makes you more heroic than a hero is the fact that you saved the husband of the woman you loved. What happened then?'

'Oh, they were grateful, very grateful to me. I simply let them be.'

'Wonderful!'

'Of course, for years my heart was raw. I had lost the woman I loved. I mean, I had to let her go.'

'Oh yes, that's sad, certainly, but think of what you did! Your sacrifice!'

Her words, her joy, her mere look crippled my blood flow, again. If then, as I appeased her with my stories, I had thought that the honesty phenomenon came with *versions*, I was wrong. But it was Valli who allowed me to live with that belief for five years, God bless her soul. At least I had those five years.

At the age of twenty, after ten years of loving me, she left. She had written a note.

Dear Mr Percy (her use of this impersonal title rather than Father made me weep)

When you took me in, I was a mere child but I knew the gravity of your kindness. I had just lost my parents but you were quick to replace them and I should thank you. But you see, when a girl reaches maturity, she can understand many things. I now know that my ten years with you were lies. You never saved the man from the python. You never helped Sita Devi. You only made her your whore. You were never a kindly manager. You abused and tortured hundreds of Indian workers, my people. Yes, Mr Percy, I know everything. I happened to be cleaning your study when I found your journals. (I have ripped out several pages for your perusal.) Then I remembered the stories my grandmother used to tell me about a monster on the plantation she worked on; a man who believed he was God because he had been born white. Yes, my grandmother was one of the 'coolies' you raped and traumatized. I cannot stand to be around such a man. It would be wrong. But I should thank you for feeding me and putting a roof over my head for the last few years.

Lastly, I hope you start to pray for your soul. Even then, I'm not sure if you can be saved.
Valli.

Some time has passed since Valli's departure. I imagine her running back to me, bursting through the doors to announce, 'I forgive you, Father. We all forgive you.' But I keep returning to her note and the pages from my journal, thinking how, when I had written down what was threatening to fossilize in my system, I had only wanted to heal. The pages remind me that the former process had already begun when I held the pen. I read those pages every day, attempting to understand, to *truly* understand them.

> I was ready to fire but in that moment the coolie turned around and I realized that it was Muthiah. Suddenly my grip on the rifle loosened and I watched the man and the python battle for survival, the so-called lord of the animal world feebly fisting the snake that had already twisted itself around the emaciated coolie form. I witnessed the most gruesome act of nature's brutality. The python opened its mouth in degrees of width and length, each stage affirming the miracles dormant within God's creatures. Muthiah met his death probably midway through the snake's body, his screams cushioned by its moist interiors. When he had died and the python could not move from the weight of its supper, I shot it.
>
> At Muthiah's funeral, Sita Devi had to be sedated and afterwards she came up to me to thank me for attempting to save her husband's life. 'They all said you shot the snake and tried to pull Muthiah out but it was too late. But thank you, Mr Percy, thank you so much for trying.' I touched her arm and told her that she didn't have to tap trees any longer. She could work for me and I imagined that in time she would finally forget Muthiah and be herself in my bed. That day never came. Two weeks after her husband's death, Sita Devi drank weed killer and died in my home. There was no suicide note. There was no need for such a thing. After that my days and nights were filled with Muthiah, Sita Devi and the python. I thought about how I had ruined the couple and the more I contemplated it, the more I found that I could not stand to be with myself. I collected more coolie women,

angered more husbands, produced more half-castes. I had also taken to forcing my women to do things they didn't want to do. All the while I pretended to be a python, coiling, crushing, consuming, and Sita Devi's face flashed on the wall above my bed.

Then the Second World War erupted, altering whatever assumptions we British had of our position in the colonies. Malaya slowly slipped away from us and the Japanese parked themselves where we had once built our legacy. Coal Island was safe in 1942 and it took those self-appointed kings of Asia a whole year to find and ruin us. When they came, my coolies and I worked with the Communists to fight the Japanese off. For once, without the plantation to shield and elevate me, I felt closer to my coolies but by then they had already begun to despise me. I tried to protect my children but the husbands threatened me with scythes. We were, however, united by the fact that we hated the Japanese and wanted them gone so we provided food and shelter to the Communists whenever we could and I fought with them, killing a host of Japanese men who I decided had cruel, upturned faces. That made me want to get rid of them all the more.

When the Japanese were finally defeated in 1945, the British were considerably weakened. I returned to my job knowing that it wouldn't be long before I was no longer needed. I thought about England but I could not go back to that life. I made up my mind to marry a local woman and make Malaya my home. I chose a simple peasant girl called Puteri Lila and she died in childbirth after a year of marriage. The baby died with her.

I spent the rest of my years teaching in a small school and

> hiding in my house when work was over. I spoke to nobody and kept a cat for company. But each year brings more troubles to my mind. Muthiah, Sita Devi and the python continue to follow me. At times I hear the screams of my women or feel their tears on my cheeks. All that's left to do is hide.

I continue to wait for Valli as I approach my hundredth year. I wonder why God has made me endure life this long, with my past weighing on my back like the python I had once allowed to satisfy its hunger. Every time I attempt to forgive myself through prayer, it comes back to me, that lustful beast, curling around my feet, telling me that nature has already decided what we are to be, some killers, others abusers and the rest, victims of their own constitution which will remain wanting until it consumes bodies, alive and intact.

Valli has left me. This life is a brewery.

4

Mushroom Universe

THE DAMN BELLS rang in my ear –TINkle, TINkle, TINkle – but I still stood and watched as he placed his hands on my best friend's head, murmuring, 'Tathva, Tathva, Tathva.' Amitabh got up from the monk's feet, tearing, his legs unsteady, his face smudged with an expression which he had been using a lot of late. I didn't know what it was. It could have been peace, fear, even apathy. TINkle. TINkle. TINkle. At least if it had alternated between TINkle and tinKLE, it wouldn't have been so bad. But I had made a promise to Amitabh's mother. I had to save her son.

Amitabh Kannan and I grew up together, mostly outside of each other's homes, even though he lived two doors down the road from me. We met at kindergarten where we began our tradition of exchanging lunchboxes. I had wanted his idli, chutney and flask of Horlicks and he had coveted my sandwich and Red Grape juice.

'You don't know how lucky you are to have such different food,' Amitabh once said to me when we were seven or eight. I wanted to say the same thing to him but he might have thought I was mocking him.

'Seriously, man,' he continued several years later, 'your mother makes killer Western feats. We live on rice and curry at home. Where's the drama? Oh and the occasional chapatti, I suppose. You know . . . from what you've been telling me, your mum, she seems free, like she doesn't care about tradition and rules and all that shit. Or how women are supposed to behave.'

'You mean just because she's lost to us after 7 p.m.? When Daddy brings home those bottles of chardonnay and they sit on the patio where she says things like, 'My darlings. Listen to the frogs croak. So utterly, wonderfully tragic? I'm looking for something else, Tabh, and I don't think I can find it in that house after dark.'

'It's funny you say that. You know what my mother does at night? She just sits on the sofa with a cup of thick Milo watching a Tamil drama. And my father? He's out having temple meetings. Do you see how limiting that all is? I'm also looking for something else and I don't think I can find it in that house after dark. What's even worse, I don't know where to look for it.'

I nodded. He was growing up to be one of those articulate men with floppy hair and sharp noses, the type that girls wanted as husbands. But we had no time for girls. We were too busy hating the rest of the world, creating our own system of existence in comic books, scientific facts, philosophy and dreams of escape. We were solemn boys, hardly ever conventionally naughty, in the sense that our crimes were motivated by desires larger than running away with a couple of doughnuts. We stayed at the back of the class and wrote notes to each other.

'The hummingbird is the only bird that can fly backwards.'

'Mars is red because of the oxide in its soil'.

At recess we would sit underneath the school's universally feared Angsana tree and go through magazines like *Science for Humanists*, *Socialism Re-read* and *Literature Review of the World*.

'Look at them,' Amitabh would say, lifting two lean fingers up in the air and directing them at groups of girls, and then at groups of boys, who were conquering the football field with their screams and momentary appropriations of titles such as 'Sultan', 'Doctor' and 'President'. 'What on earth do they think they're doing? Wasting their youth, that's what. Do they even care about shit? Hell lah, they *are* shit. And what's the point of being so holy? Girls with the girls. Boys with the boys. Is there anything more insulting?'

'Sure, Tabh,' I'd reply, 'they don't even know that they might as well throw away their watches.'

Things got worse in the classroom.

Once, Amitabh asked Mr Jusang, the history teacher, 'Why is it that we only have three pages on that big world event, the Renaissance, and fifty-five pages on how Malacca became Malacca? I mean, we *know* that already. Since I was nine, Mr Jusang, and now I'm fourteen, I've heard that story over and over again. But you see, we don't *know* about the Renaissance. I'm not sure about the rest, but I'm quite keen to find out how those people got to be four-in-one chaps. I mean, what do *you* know about the Renaissance, Mr Jusang?'

Later that day, the headmistress had 'words' with Amitabh and he, refusing, of course, to understand why 'why' questions should be limited to one or two once in a while, declared the whole business of school invalid. He still went, but he was never really *there*.

We began, as Amitabh put it, 'flicking' books from various libraries across the island. But we soon read all the books that were worth our time. Then we started visiting homes and flicking books from there. 'It's all good,' Amitabh said, 'what are we doing at the end of the day? Educating ourselves in our own way. I just want to *know*.'

I suppose this was when our truancy began which affected Amitabh in ways that would, in the end, change his perceptions – in a smack and a bang or two – into entities that no one else could access.

'Sheldon,' he said to me on a dull day in the park, 'I brought us something.'

An exceptional clarity swooshed out from his eyes and I could tell that he had created a plan for us. Perhaps a new method of studying novels or dense mathematical equations. Just the other day we agreed that we'd need a guide book to help us read Newton's *Principia Mathematica*.

'But before I show you,' he continued, 'I want to ask you something.'

'Go ahead,' I said, 'but if it's about Newton's idea of time, I still don't get it. And I don't know how Einstein corrected it.'

'Don't worry. I can promise that you'll understand time after this. You'll really see that we've got time all wrong. Clocks are just stupid. Anyway, here it is. What do you think of this place, Coal Island?'

I had never left Coal Island before, so I replied, 'Well, it's home, isn't it? What's more to say?'

'Dig deeper, man. What do you see around you? What are those trees? What is the beach, the sea? Who are those people? Are they real? Is Coal Island just another piece of land on this earth? Or is it its own kind of place like no other?'

He had probably woken up that morning with philosophy and disgust trailing behind him, still unable to return to whatever dreamscape they had come from. Amitabh asked crazy, impossible questions when the bleakness that dazzled his mind zoomed in on the visible world. Then he demanded, like He-Man or Lion-o giving out orders, that those insipid layers be ripped off. It was not that I didn't recognize puzzles and futility in the world. I saw them but knew that it would be absurd to pine for answers or a change. But Amitabh would say in a deep, morose voice, 'That's what I'm saying. Absurd is right. It's all so ridiculous.' He would spend the rest of the day in silence, thinking about the giant joke of our existence.

'Tabh, are you feeling absurd again?'

'No, listen man. Just tell me. What are the components of Coal Island?'

'I don't know,' I said although I was thinking about the question quite seriously.

'It's just atoms. None of this is real. We can transcend this place.'

'Okay. How?'

'I like that you're still asking these questions, Sheldon. Look,' he said as he produced a plastic bag from his backpack, 'these will take you there.'

He picked a spongy mushroom from the bag and flashed it in my face.

'A mushroom. So, this is what it's become, is it? Now even vegetables can do things.'

'Magic,' he said, his face shining from some unknowable light and I realized that the mushrooms were not the kind my mother stuffed with peppered rice.

'What will happen?' I asked, suddenly feeble and defeated by the manic joy in his grin.

'Sheldon, I am looking for the truth. There is only one and I don't care what the postmodernists are saying. Out of many is a single, simple truth and I'm going to find it. You know that writer, Huxley, he said that drugs can help us enter the dimension of truth.'

Hell, man. He even took the drugs to prove it.

I checked out the mushroom, blown away that it carried within its cap and stem the capacity for that much truth.

'Okay,' I said, 'Huxley was a clever man. Let's do it.'

We made a soil-tasting tea from the mushrooms and drank it in his room. Within minutes the grey walls turned bright and yellow light jet-sailed through and out of the bricks. The interiors of objects, from the rugged office chair to the table fan, leapt out of their bodies, totally nudifying their anatomies. Strips of light travelled up and down their systems like bullet-speed elevators. Transparency made sense. Sight was malleable like glob or goo or flubber. Sober-vision, created by the brain through society, cowered behind images, shit-scared of the whip that was cunningly tucked away in a secret duct. But we had jumped over the whip. We saw the inner lives of things, the satisfying bazooka-death of matter, the revival of the unseeable which then, for me anyway, in my tripped out state, was lucid and most definitely present. Flinging a hand seemed like a slow-mo act, the karate kid taking his time to wow his audience. Slow, slow, slowly did we vibrate in that state, having forgotten the beginning and the end, if they ever even existed. It was a gold-dust dimension. The glitter made us stop.

It took hours for the effects of the tea to wear off and when they did, Amitabh and I looked at each other. He said, 'What did Einstein say?'

'That time is not linear.'

We were fifteen and finding that science wasn't strictly book-bound was an awesome epiphany for us, quite different from the realization that the game of football catered only to some.

Every day after our first tryst with the vegetable, Amitabh insisted on entering the world of torpedo cups and disco colour. In the beginning, it was all I could think of.

When we sat at the beach the next day, after holding our hands up in saint-or-beauty queen fashion to Mrs Sarimah and Mrs Kumaran who were standing dangerously close to the beach road and obviously exchanging crucial information about so-and-so, Amitabh whipped out a jumbo steel flask – the kind manual labourers and tuition-goers bet their lives on, and we drank to our new existence. I could see the two ladies adjusting their sight so that one eye sneakily shifted towards us and the other remained on the matter at hand: a slut's elopement, some fool's extramarital affair, arsenic cupcakes eaten at a friend's house. But what could they say about us? We weren't puffing at a cigarette or guzzling a can of beer. We were, as far as they were concerned, indulging in a dose of Ceylon/Earl Grey/English Breakfast tea, made for the bored, ready-to-be-seduced housewife who suffers from mysterious panic attacks or the office worker who thinks that life was made for the 3 p.m. tea break (yeah, Coal Island has plenty of those).

Living on an island, a small island, means that your senses become sharp. You smell the bitch-sting in a concerned neighbour's voice: 'Oh, Josie, Josie,' said Eveline Lopez to my mother, 'my boy got the highest mark in mathematics in the entire school. Your son need any help? Looks like my boy can start giving tuition. Hor Hor Hor.' You watch how eyes suddenly light up or go all fizzy when a face droops from humiliation. The ears can hear a woman sobbing for her life ten miles away. Most of all, after the senses have zapped into themselves what they must, news spreads.

If Mrs Sarimah and her sidekick had witnessed us lighting up or juggling a bottle of whisky, the whole of Coal Island would have known about the demonhood of the Kannan boy and his supposedly docile friend (ha!), the D'Cruz boy, who at the age of fifteen had already mastered the art of debauched escapism, something that should only afflict a person once they entered the real world – the real world of making money, tying the knot (read: a knot around the neck) and procreating, that is. I suppose it never dawned on the collection of aunties on the island (this group was a bombastic one of no-joke proportions) that getting away from the facile, the gruesome and the downright horrid can be found right within nature, in the bushes, in fact, by a field where their sons played makeshift football and their daughters made ropes out of rubber bands and skipped away their juvenile worries (whatever they were; probably something to do with a Barbie's missing head).

Amitabh had done his research on the Internet. 'Go Beyond For Free', was the website, an offshoot of 'Food For Free'. A tiny, almost invisible link lay at the bottom of the site and Amitabh, like Superman desperate to fly above what he saw around him, found the words quite easily and clicked away to an ironical freedom. Of course, then, irony was too unreal a concept, even for us, who had dished out our minds, something certain geriatrics never get a chance to do.

For me the tea had always just been a chance to get at anatomies, for a short while. When the effects wore off I could accept that the chair was the chair it had been before it lifted off the ground and did unchair-like acrobatics until, finally, it disappeared into the air and reincarnated into a throne. The fact that the light bulb, no longer a basket of stars, reshaped into a glass pear with a dead filament didn't depress me. But for Amitabh, going back into the world of matter was a pain in the arse, a struggle, I would say, against his own nature. When he used to suggest drinking more tea after we were sober, I said okay at first because I hated him sober. His eyes fluttered less, his mood crashed to find company with microorganisms and he utterly butchered beauty. 'Look how the leaves rot,' he said to me one day, responding to my claim that there were more green leaves than brown ones, 'eventually, they wither away and die'. It was impossible to talk to him then about anything. The best conversations we had were at the point between complete elevation and sobriety when he could actually speak about the things he had seen and was seeing.

'The distance between you and me is nil,' he said.

'Yes, there seems to be nothing separating us. I see all the colours of the rainbow too. Do you?'

'Ya. It's like God came down and gave the world a boost. The sea, Shel, look at it. It's like a membrane of light.'

'Shit man, it's like Coal Island's become a different place.'

'That's what I was asking you before. What's this island to you? Is it what we see or something else? I mean if we dig deep, we see everything inside it. Its light, its truth, beyond all the asinine things people make up for it. Now it's stark. Pure light and colour.'

Hours later, my eyes normal again, I somehow kept the ecstasy – the sheer orgasm – of seeing Coal Island as a place beyond the categories people dirtied it with. Market. Bus station. School. Post Office. *Inside* those entities were pixels of light and God. When Ms Kartika who worked at the post office cursed me for using saliva instead of gum to stick my stamps, I smiled at her and thought about the pixels.

'Shel,' Amitabh said to me one day, 'do you see how mushrooms and school don't gel? You've got to choose, man. You can't sit in Madam Moniza's maths class and watch an 8 walk out of the blackboard and sit on your desk.' I mean, you can't say, 'Madam Moniza, one of your 8s has pitched a tent on my desk. It's staring at me and I've told it many times to go back to the blackboard but no, it just won't go. What's the best way to talk to an 8?' See what I mean, Shel? Now if you ask me, I'd rather be taught by Sir Mushroom than by that pock-faced fool. What do you say?'

I thought about it. We had judged school a long time ago. But it was a mere judgement. Now he was suggesting transforming that judgement into an actuality. I couldn't. I was not that kind of a radical (I mean, I wanted experiences just as much as Amitabh did but, hell, what's the point of going through life wasted?)

'I see what you mean but, Tabh, that's a little loony, don't you think? At some point, we've got to get through school. Think of it as a damn dumb rite of passage. You can always drink your tea as soon as the school bell rings.'

'When have I ever been a hypocrite? No, no, Shel, you do what you like but I'm staying with Sir Shroom. See how beautiful that sounds?'

'And when they start asking questions about where you are, then what the hell do I do?'

'Oh, come on now, Shel. Don't best friends lie for each other?'

'I thought only hypocrites lied.'

'I'm not *really* being a hypocrite. This is a small island and all . . . oh, please, Shel, you know what I'm talking about,' he said, pausing for a moment to stare at something that was clearly a foil for cerebration. 'Okay,' he resumed, 'here's a compromise. I'll make occasional appearances.'

I left it at that.

Soon enough, the teachers started questioning his absence. But I was ready with my battalion of excuses.

He was having chronic vomiting after an unfortunate bout of clam-eating.

He had twisted his wrist while pounding mustard seeds and fenugreek for his mother.

He was fixing the stand fan when he got mildly but significantly electrocuted.

The big government exam, PMR, was approaching and although I understood Amitabh's mad quest to discover the soul of the universe, I myself went potty wondering if he could answer questions such as 'What are the twenty-six moral values in life?' or 'If Ah Chong finds a wallet in the bus station, what should he do?' (He never liked Moral Studies.)

I would find him lying on a rug by the sea with his eyes fixed on the sky. He had found a cranny tucked away from the laser eyes of society and it was up to me to make sure that he was clean before he returned home. Often, I snatched the flask away and when he protested, I said, 'Sure, go on drinking the tea and when you face your mother, what'll you say? Ma, I've found the light? You *know* she'll *know* something's up. Just stay cool for now, Tabh. There's always tomorrow morning.' My words frightened me, I have to admit. The tea-sessions were expanding like an occupied womb, without an obvious sense of growth. Then, he started surrendering the flask on his own. 'Good job, Tabh,' I said, creeped out by the condition of his eyes. They were large, the pupils somewhat zigzagged, but I took them to be part of what the mushrooms' curse could do. When the flask started missing and his eyes still looked like damn hibiscus flowers, I demanded a confession. 'You can't expect me to believe that you're not high on something,' I said, 'come on, tell me, what are you taking? There's no flask here. There must be something else.'

'You're not getting all prude-y on me are you, Shel? You've got to expand . . . you know, what's the funniest thing about horizons? The closer you get to them, the further away they are. So you've got to mix it up. Try new things. Find new ways.'

He had discovered more ingredients for his transformation into a creature, a Gollum, waiting at the sides. He hovered in the air like a hummingbird sizing up its flower, a column of space separating the two, except that the bird does, in the end, enter its temporary home. Amitabh stayed away, watching. There was cocaine, small doses of heroin (he admitted to being afraid of its long-term consequences which included mental and emotional numbness) and marijuana when he felt he needed a break from the more substantial stuff.

'And where are you getting the money for your experiments?' I had to ask him one day.

'No need for such questions. The universe provides,' he said, but days later he confessed that he had been regularly taking RM 50 notes from his father's jam-packed wallet.

Then I started wondering about the state of his body, how he looked *inside*, how wild his organs must have been, trying to work but tired, perhaps surrounded by a fog of drug-dust since his skin was becoming lighter, less showy with blood. When my father had a heart attack, after a lifetime of inking his body with wine and whisky, also great trucks that went to different worlds, I began thinking vertically, not horizontally, about the heart that worked like Sisyphus, about the moral liver, frantic for cleanliness, pushing away gunk. I drew spliced open bodies that revealed a system that flowed like a thoughtless stream but which, when pried into, was complex in its tubes and routes and functions. I had no choice. I would have to pay Amitabh's mother a visit.

'Auntie,' I said to her when she opened the front door with a look of bedazzlement on her face, 'can I come in?'

She admitted me in like the bloody Queen of Sheba agreeing to listen to her minion's apology.

'Sorry to bother you, Auntie, but I need to tell you something important.'

'Your mother is drunk at home?' she said with a vicious smirk.

I wanted to get the hell out of there, to let her discover her son's suicide on her own. But I remembered Amitabh.

'No. This is not about my family. Actually, Amitabh . . .'

She looked at the Persian carpet. I could tell that she knew something but she wasn't quite sure what.

'Auntie, maybe this is not so easy to say.'

'Please, if you know something, you must tell me. I don't know what has happened to that boy. We cannot talk to him anymore. At first I thought you made him . . . made him . . . like this.'

She began weeping.

I said, 'Your son is taking drugs. Drugs, Auntie.'

She stared at me, and said in a black voice, 'So it has come to this.'

For the next few weeks I did not see Amitabh. His parents locked him indoors and the Queen of Sheba fed him shitloads of food, and he went through cold sweats, nightmares – all sorts – until he resurfaced fatter, larger-eyed, but still glum. We never spoke about my talk with his mother. And when the PMR exam came, I collected five A-s. Amitabh wagged his results sheet in the air, saying, 'You see, Shel? Not going to school means that you get the full load. Seven bloody A-s. Shouldn't someone tell them that something's wrong here?'

For a year-and-a-half after that, we attended the final years of secondary school, discussed our ideas in the afternoons and remained sober. Somewhat. Well, I was but Amitabh, finding life traumatic without his old companions, found new ones. He started drinking beer and I was a hundred per cent cool with it since that was like giving up mutton for chicken. There were times of course when drunkenness became a problem but he still managed to ace the SPM exams. He was featured in the Coal Island newspapers as one of the twelve students who scored straight A-s in the country. Who cared that he'd been drunk during a few papers?

When we were at college Amitabh rocked with the girls. I could see that he was handsome but that didn't immediately mean that he had veto power. Or maybe it did. There was something else in him – a kind of sleek energy – that cornered girls and made them his own, including my sister but I was too busy being a brother to Amitabh to notice. I'd only find out when it was too late. In any case, college was his thing. For the first time, the subjects got him excited. 'There are a million atoms crawling about on one strand of hair!' he said one morning and then, on another, 'The gene pool is a place of fixed possibilities!' Sure he had beer on his breath but unlike the other drugs, that wasn't stopping him from being the best. Amitabh did well consistently, helping me, always the lesser boy, along the way, but I didn't mind. I was no pack leader.

We both got into medical school in India after two years at college. I was beginning to think that Amitabh had dropped his penchant for cutting open the world and looking deep into its light. But it was India that broke him again. The problem there was that drugs were cheap, accessible, too common. Students absorbed them like coffee and went on crazy bike rides around the infested streets, charging at stalls, yahooing at the colours of cakes and grains and saris. Amitabh was electrified. The issue I had with his new phase of drug-taking was that he had stopped talking about looking for the truth or the soul of the universe. This time, he had given up on philosophy in favour of fun – riding with the boys, cavorting with the girls, whistling at cats, laughing at inanimate objects. I caught him one day staring at a vase and mumbling something about darkness.

'What did you say?' I asked.

He looked up at me, sad, fearful, his hair sweaty and uncombed. 'Sit with me a while, Shel.'

I sat, feeling that I had never caught this particular mood of his before.

'You know, Shel, I was so stupid before. I thought everyone went through it. Like a rite of passage. Now I know that it's only for certain people.'

'What do you mean?'

'Ah, well. I don't know if I should feel embarrassed. This whole thing makes me out to be weak.'

'I don't think there's anything wrong with weakness. Everyone's got something.'

'You ever feel low, like really low so that it's not lowness that you feel after a while but nothing at all?'

I thought about it. I didn't quite understand him.

'Not so much. More like I can feel down sometimes. I don't know what nothing feels like.'

'You're lucky, then. Damn it, Sheldon. I never knew, all those years . . . something hollow, just air waiting to be filled, no atoms, just nothing, then the mushrooms, oh they came at the perfect time, I could see things again. Then this thing – this empty air – would return. Funny thing is, the emptiness was wild. It could go on and on, unchecked. I didn't even know when it was coming and when it came I got so used to it that I thought it was normal but now I think, well, no. We're not supposed to feel nothing.'

I had not known. Years of friendship and I had not known. 'It's okay, Tabh. Actually, many people go through this. It's just that nobody wants to talk about it. There's plenty of help around.'

The next day I made an appointment for him with the university psychiatrist and he was given little oval pills to take three times a day. No alcohol, said the doctor and Amitabh, disgusted by the instruction, threw the strips of medication into the bin.

'Come on, Tabh. You've got to do *something*. Look, I've even made a list of movie stars who have what you have,' I said. At times, I thought that I was making sense but the high-pitched laughter that came after made me feel like a damn quack doctor.

And then, after three years of battling with him, his condition, his incessant drug-taking and wild, craggy behaviour, he stepped into my room on a quiet night and announced, 'Sheldon, I've been thinking. You're right lah, man. It's been going on for too long. I'm giving up the drugs for a new life. I want to get better.'

The words, which I had always imagined would be spat out after years of abuse when his face had shrivelled into a ball of drug-tinted leather, captured me, made me feel heroic, like a goddamn real doctor.

'That's right, Shel. I've been doing some research. There are many, many alternatives to the pills. Some say diet and meditation. Some say exercise and healthy distractions. Then I found this site. Chant your way through life. Every utterance brings you closer towards God, to shedding earthly issues. I'm going back to Malaysia and becoming a Buddhist.'

There was no way of stopping him. He had answers for all my questions. Becoming a doctor, he said, was only a mortal ambition. God could not be relegated to the periphery. His air was certainly being filled up. He had become the opposite of what he had been before.

He left the next week and three months later I received two entirely different phone calls from Malaysia, regarding Amitabh. The first was from Mrs Kannan.

'Sheldon,' she said softly, 'Sorry to disturb you like this lah, boy, but you see, something is not quite right here. Ami . . . Amitabh, he, I mean, I know I should be happy the boy's got into religion but . . . he . . . well, it doesn't seem right. He doesn't say a word to us. Only writes on paper. He says he is on a vow of silence. He doesn't eat. Only a few nuts in one day. He sleeps on the porch outside. People are talking, boy. I . . . I . . . don't know what to do. Maybe he will listen to you. Please help us. My only son, you know.'

The second phone call came from my mother.

'Sheldon,' she said, 'listen to me. That bloody bastard friend of yours, come back here and sort him out. Oh god, son. How was I to know with that orange robe of his and shaven head that he could be such a scoundrel? Chanting and silence, it seems. Bloody rotten liar! Daisy is pregnant. That's right, son, she's got a nice little half-Indian bun in the oven. Please, dear, just take some time off and come back. For a while. God knows we need you here. And your father has started drinking again.'

I returned to Coal Island a few days later, not knowing what to think of the situation. Was he putting on various shows according to his changing temperament? Or was he capable of honestly performing each one – Buddhist in the daytime, lover at night? A showgirl-showboy prancing around on a stage. I guess most brothers would have felt angry at that point but I didn't. Amitabh had layers of desire, determination, desperation in him that were intricate and were always threatening to clash. In the beginning, they collided only within him and nobody saw the implosion except me, but now they had stretched wider and were polluting others.

I found him in a small terrace house, chanting and hairless. The chanting continued for hours and I waited, hoping that I would catch him looking at me but he never once moved his sight from the floor. Amitabh, I wanted to say, look at yourself, man. When it ended I went up to him. It didn't take long for his vow of silence to be broken. 'I've missed you,' he said.

'Buddhists are not supposed to miss things or people,' I replied.

He smiled and led me out of the house. 'You must have heard but listen, Shel, that was when I first returned and my faith was not so strong. I'm really sorry for everything but I'm celibate now. I'm going to become a monk. Listen, I have to go now. We're going down to the sea to swim for healing and cleansing.'

He walked away and didn't turn back when I said, 'But you can't swim!'

I followed them to the beach. One by one they descended, chanting. Orange robes billowed in the water, filling up with air – Amitabh's air I thought, that had once been free of atoms. The deep tenor voices accompanied the floating fabric and I thought of a sun that had melted into the sea. In a way I could see the attraction to this – the peace that comes with prayer and rituals.

And then I heard the flapping and Amitabh's choked voice. He was drowning but the chanting continued. I ran into the water, pushing through the chanters as I searched for him but there were just too many people in my way. I kept swimming and pulling at legs but still the chanting carried through the air. I thought, that's it. He will drown in this mass of orange, in this vulgar clump of bodies and minds that prefer to reach God through stampedes rather than by ordinary meditation. I dipped my head into the water several times but I saw nothing except bodies in motion, legs kicking, alive. I doubled up my free-style. What if he was already dead? Who would console Mr and Mrs Kannan? Then there was Daisy and the unborn baby. I swam harder, beating the waves, thinking that I would swim all the way to the horizon if I had to, that horizon which we had wanted to cross when we were boys. Beyond it was what we, Amitabh in particular, had sought: the inside of life or as he had once said, 'What this thing is made of. The light, the colour, the atoms of ourselves and this place.'

Then something tugged at my foot. I turned my body around and there he was, limp, almost gone but desperate to go on.

I stayed by his side at the hospital even after his parents had left. The doctor said that he would survive and I wanted to be there when he opened his eyes. All night I watched him, the man who looked so much like a boy now, defeated many times, but kept awake by the promise that the horizon would crack open.

He awoke the next morning, still weak but keen to talk. 'Looking good, Shel.'

'Well, I should say that to you. You're like a regenerating worm.'

'Ha. I am a bit of a survivor, aren't I?'

'Maybe too much.'

'Oh and thanks for dragging me out, man. Don't think drowning is the right kind of death for me. I deserve something more noble. Like kidney failure.'

'Ya, you're made for better things. How you feeling?'

'Like I've drunk the sea but other than that, something else too. Something nicer. Let's call it clarity.'

'Near-death clarity. Sometimes these things are positive, you know.'

'Yes. Last night I dreamt of many things. They weren't normal dreams. More like insights. I'm not meant to be a doctor, Shel, or a monk. The drugs were bringing me down. I'm still looking. But then again, I've always been looking. Is that a bad thing?'

'Not everyone knows what they want. In fact, if you ask me, it's those who never know and who keep looking who are the honest ones, or at least they're more interesting than dullards like me.'

'Ha. I think I know what I am, actually. I am like a gene pool. Full of fixed possibilities.'

He closed his eyes and whispered, 'Fixed possibilities.'

He was getting closer to his horizon.

5

Flame of the Forest

'ROSEY! AFTER SO long hah! And here you are, still.'

Some members are capable of saying this once a week. Monday: Gym, dinner, bar. Tuesday: Tennis, dinner, playground, bar. Wednesday: Squash, dinner, bar. Thursday: Drama practice, dinner, bar. Friday: Society meeting, dinner, bar. Saturday and Sunday: Bar. Then the words roll out like spiders being purged from the mouth: 'Rosey! After so long hah! And here you are, still.' I could have said, 'Monday, Tuesday, Wednesday and Thursday I serve you fish and chips with extra tartar sauce. Friday, it is pork pie with thousand island sauce. On weekends, I bring you finger foods every hour. I am here and so are you.' But they are members of the Coal Island Recreational Club, built in 1903 by Colonel Gregory Hunter III, Governor of the island. From across the road, the club is woody, quiet, history. Even the fans in this building are no longer sold in electrical shops in town.

I nod, 'Yes, yes, I am still here. So long and always will be.'

When the children from ten, twenty years ago – now men and women – return for a holiday from Ireland, Russia, England, Egypt, nearly doctors and lawyers like their parents, they might say, 'Auntie Rose, you're here. How wonderful!' That's how it's done. It must be the countries, so far away from here, that have taught them how to talk and bend their heads, when to smile, laugh, and where to put their full-stops. I've seen you drool, I would have liked to say, I might have even burped you and when I used to sit in the WC during my five-minute break, I changed your nappies when your mothers were dripping fat in the sauna. But how many times does a young adult need to hear about their uselessness as a baby? I say, 'Wonderful, yes, it's wonderful that you are here too.' Sometimes they bring me fridge magnets. I have Russian dolls, a California seaside, the Eiffel Tower, two Egyptian pyramids, the San Francisco bridge. Imagine: these items had once been in all those countries, sitting in shops, hearing languages that come out like random nonsense, held by hands that work because of food I'd never known. This is a kind of travelling, I think to myself when I open my bag of magnets and look at them.

Out there is a world.

It's the men and women, the fathers and mothers who bother me. I have watched them grow old and brown, licking the drinks I served them off their lips, shrieking after the third or fourth, calling out, 'Rosey Sayang, one more!' I told them many times that my name is not Rosey. It's Roseleana Binti Abdul Khamis. Rose is fine, not Rosey. But they like to stretch my name out to show how comfortable and blessed they are at the club, the place they go to for everything, their heaven: a slab of steak, a Bloody Mary and a ping pong ball. Hah . . .

I applied for the job twenty-five years ago, in the eighties, when I was seventeen and pregnant with Suhana. I had passed SPM with a third grade and the very next day, after Ibu and Ayah were so relieved that I hadn't failed, I began vomiting. Into the flowerpot. In the kitchen sink. Into my coffee cup. On the cat. I could never make it to the toilet in time and Ayah thought that I might have been poisoned by somebody jealous of my fair skin. 'How many times people notice that you look like half-orange *putih*? Someone's not happy about this,' he concluded. But the doctor had different news. Ayah became purple. This is no exaggeration. Little dark veins popped up on his usually cream-pink face, and turned him into a morning glory. He demanded to know the boy's name which I gave, knowing that Hisham had already left for Kuala Lumpur. 'I'll kill him. I'll kill him,' Ayah said but Hisham was weaving his way through the faraway city, bumping into, as I often daydreamed, Malay women with skirts and bum-length hair, their faces lit by neon lights. Hisham had told me when we were at school, 'You're the only girl I'll ever love. We'll get married after SPM.' On the day of the final paper, he took me to the car shed and held my hand tightly and I thought yes, this is my moment, he is going to propose, but instead, he said, 'Ling, I feel too young to just stay on the island. I'm going to Kuala Lumpur. Come with me.' I quietly removed my hand from his and walked away. I only cried when I was back in my room. He never came after me or tried to persuade me to follow him. He just left a note saying, 'I'll be back. Wait for me.' He did not return.

The pregnancy led me to the club. I was the eldest of five children and Ayah's fisherman's wages were already too little for us. Ibu did try to help out by selling *nasi lemak* and *kuih* but she never brought back much. One day I was walking back from the beach where I always went when I couldn't stand myself and needed to be reminded that I was still worth the limbs, heart and liver that I had. I saw a poster on the wall of the Coal Island Recreational Club: 'Waitress Wanted. Apply Within.' I did and got the job instantly. 'Must be your fair skin,' Ayah said and I replied perhaps, although I did have muscular fingers and stony elbows which meant that I had the stamina to hang my arms, crooked, in the air for many minutes, even half an hour. Balancing plates was never a problem.

The club then was not very different from what it is now. It's built entirely from wood and all around the building is a single balcony, lined with pots of anthuriums, watched from above by baskets of orchids. The ceilings are low, capable of making you feel as though you're in a baby's cot or a coffin, depending on the day, the night, the mood you've been put into, and the breeze is almost always around, mixing into the interiors from the sea. Close to the beach where the sailing yachts are stored is a Flame of the Forest tree which Puna, the other long-time waitress, told me about in my first week of work. 'We all love to go to the tree when we can before anyone can shout, "One more Guinesssss!" Someone said it's old, one of the oldest things on the island. It's not simply-simply there, you know. Just go and see. Sit there for a while and tell me after what you find out.' A mystery tree, I thought, ignoring a call from the far end of the dining hall for a squeeze of lime on a plate of noodles. I sat under it and not knowing what I was supposed to harvest there, I trembled. Is that what the tree does to you? Puna gasped. 'Chi-chi,' she said, 'no lah. Not nervous. The head should clear. The tree takes out head-knots.' Next time then. The tree will undo my head-knots next time. Puna said it was probably because I was new. The tree had not understood my musk yet so it was important to keep visiting it, airing armpits, opening legs (just a bit lah), running around it, sweating. 'How long you been here?' I asked her after the tree had made me anxious. 'One year only. Here you know who comes? To this club? Haiiiii! Roseleana! Got even PRINCES! Lot of opportunity. We lucky here. Very lucky.' That was all I needed. A clear, enthusiastic affirmation from a person who had worked there for at least twelve months and wasn't dying.

So it went on . . .

Puna and I, a comfortable double act, in and out of the kitchen, the bathroom, the storeroom, the gamesroom, wiping, filling, serving, regularly guiding the whisky, wine and cocktail drinkers to their cars, fearing their journey home until noon the next day when they were beaming red and ready to begin again. Years were completed like a simple race at a sports event, the start creating the same pace as the finish, but different in nature. What happens in between is a flash, and memory, as far as I know, is not so kind to speed. Of course there was slow motion too. The flash was stretched out in front of those funny mirrors at carnivals and that's when I went to the Flame of the Forest tree and hoped that the head-knots would come loose. But they didn't . . .

'Five years already,' I once said to Puna, 'and *still* it doesn't know me? You fooling me or what, Pun?'

'No, no,' she replied, 'I tell you, everyone says they feel light in the head after they sit there. All becomes clear. Maybe you don't have head-knots?'

'Hah! You joking, is it? One small child. Eight people to feed. RM800 a month. Now my child is asking, "Bu, why I don't have Ayah?" I think so my knots are too big for the tree.'

'Could be you're not ready.'

'Ready? Ready for what?'

But Puna was already skipping away towards a customer.

Fifteen years participated in that sports event but the fifteenth year ended with more twisted oomph. Suhana became my colleague.

'Wah your daughter so grown up already, ah, and *so* pretty!' Coach Tan said. He was the Club's tennis coach. But unlike me, he was not a Club employee. Once he was done at the courts, he sat at the corner of the bar and drank Screwdrivers until his wife, Angelina, arrived and said, shamelessly, 'Tan ah! Stupid fool! Drink like this how can be strong tonight? I already told you no more drinks if you want to be a man. Haiyah! Where got husband like this one?

So . . . so . . . *lembik*!' She always allowed him to finish off his drink before catching his arm and dragging him out. But he'd be back the next day and she too returned with almost the same lines as if they were acting in a play that carries on being staged even though the audience doesn't care. A few years ago I didn't mind him or his wife or their daily bar scenes. I could laugh at them with the other waitresses, especially Puna, who was always looking for idiotic Club members as material for her storytelling sessions with her dying mother who managed to postpone death for sometime due, according to Puna, to her need for, as they called it, 'Club Tales'. (But even strong characters like Coach and Angelina Tan can't beat multiple organ failure. She died three years ago at the age of ninety-nine.)

It was on a bright afternoon when Coach Tan stopped amusing us. I was carrying a Gin and Tonic to Mr Percy Punter who came to the Club to drink alone and in hiding. He had been a regular for forty years and had chosen a bench by the beach behind a large casuarina tree to have his drinks and his dusk-time plate of potato wedges. He never spoke to anybody and I heard rumours that he hadn't been a very nice man when he was working on the rubber plantations in the olden days. But he was always polite to me and gave me tips, unlike the other Club members. As I was walking back from Mr Percy's bench, I heard voices coming from the men's WC which was meant to be used only for special functions. I thought, bloody Indonesian builders, can't they just urinate in the open like normal foreign workers? But when I opened the door I saw Coach Tan rubbing the thighs of a boy who looked a bit confused. Neither one realized that I was there and I ran back to Puna who said, 'No use. Better not tell anyone lah, Rose. They might think you're spreading lies. This Coach Tan got power here, you know. Nobody will believe you. After all, who are you in this Club?' After that, before I brought Coach Tan his Screwdriver, I cleared my throat and dumped whatever my mouth didn't want into his drink. It was my way of finding a new amusement.

It was a slow drift. Or perhaps it was happening so quickly that I hadn't noticed it, like how the earth is actually a spinning lunatic but we think that we are the only ones who are moving. I had my fingers stained with ketchup and fritters, even ham and beer, for Suhana to grow away from it, to have her ambitions elsewhere – an office, a school, a hospital if life will allow a waitress access to those places, through what she had been capable enough to produce: a child with a sharp brain. But Suhana was beautiful too; good bones, better skin, light eyes. The day she vomited into a shoe, I knew. I had brought her into the trap I was in. The trap tightened when she started working at the Club for the future of her unborn baby.

What was I to do? Let my child think that grandparents are parents and that grandparents are myths? I had to take her to the Club when she was young so that I could see her jumping about the grounds and building sandcastles, eating sandwiches and playing Police & Thief with the Club children. I had to see her learn how to swim in the pool with the help of the swimming instructor, Desmond Pullendran. (I refused Coach Tan's offer to teach her tennis, for obvious reasons.)

And when she started school, I had to witness her homework-afternoons and the way she floated in the pool with her toes stiff in the air because this, that, everything was a part of her creation, of what I had done and had to follow through.

Could it have been Kak Ain who had the clearest intuition? She was, after all, a regular Flame of the Forest visitor. She said, 'Roseleana, must be careful lah. You see your girl. How come you let her wear normal swimsuit? No shame, ah? Muslims must always cover up. Get her one of those long-sleeve, full-length costumes lah. We may work here but doesn't mean that we have to be like them. Showing leg, neck, armpit as if free show only.' I had never felt more fake or guilty or violent but I didn't know where to show those feelings, if they had any right to be seen.

Then Suhana turned fifteen and the members' sons studied her legs and arms, whispering to each other, grinning, and I took Kak Ain's advice and bought Suhana a wetsuit. Still, boys watched her and I knew that she was aware of their eyes but not once did I see her talking to any of them. Ah, I thought, I must have taught her well. No more silly girls getting cheated by boys in *this* family. Years ago when Suhana began asking questions about her father I said, 'Oh, your poor Ayah. We were high school sweethearts and we got married right after SPM. Then he got hit by a lorry and died. So sad.' She said okay and I became moral again, if I ever was. She didn't need to know that such things were possible. Let her have a door, I thought, that blocked in rules of behaviour. Wash your plate after eating. Say goodnight to your elders. Don't pick your nose, in public or in private.

Boys are only for your twenties and can be touched after marriage. Before marriage, walk at least two feet away from them. Pray as you have been born to do.

Of course I didn't know then why Suhana never spoke to any of the boys. To me, she was sitting behind the door with her string of rules for companions. But her mind was on other things – a person, in fact – and all the boys had to wait around the edges, hoping that she would, one day, look their way.

'So you're vomiting,' I said to her and she looked at me as if to say, I know you know but can we just pretend for now that we both don't know. But I wasn't prepared for delays.

'Who is it?' I asked, remembering my father all those years ago, but I didn't threaten to kill anybody. I genuinely wanted to know.

'No one who is going to be a father,' she said and then vomited again, this time on the welcome mat.

'Just tell me who. I'm not letting this happen again.'

But she refused, acting as though she were keeping a secret for this boy, and throughout her pregnancy, she kept up that aloofness although it was obvious that the child was making her uncomfortable, not physically, but in some other, more important way.

I asked Puna, '*Now* you think the tree will take me?'

'Who knows? I hope so. Go and see.'

I sat at its foot, looking out at the sea in high-tide, its waves beating against the wall that separated the Club from the beach. I closed my eyes, thinking that meditation came through a shutting out of the world that could be seen with the pupil, the iris, the cornea and whatever else that was in the eye which I had failed to remember from my schooldays. I heard the sea, the flapping of faraway wings, the crashing of mini-durians from the casuarina tree. For a moment, it was true, the head-knots were gone. I opened my eyes and wondered if there was a point to their short disappearance. Nothing had changed. 'I think,' I said to Puna, 'you've all been exaggerating lah. Not much can come from this tree. Only a bit of silence or calmness here and there. But that's it.'

Finally, Suhana's child was born. He was the colour of a candlenut – beige more than white – and had small eyes like Mrs Chan who sold vegetables at the market. Ibu and Ayah pretended not to notice the insignificant detail of his eyes. But I marked it. They even ignored Suhana's wailing when the baby was handed over to her by the nurse. But I marked it. I don't know what Ibu and Ayah really felt when Suhana was born but when I saw Rahman for the first time I looked away and imagined that he wasn't my grandson, just a baby, any baby, in a maternity ward full of babies . . .

As he grew up, and when he could say 'Bibu, Baba, Chachu, Mamee', I clapped and decided to forget about the day when he was wrapped in a white blanket and I picked him up from the hospital cot, his eyes blinking hard. I let him be my grandson even when he turned four and his face changed. At *kenduris*, questions were asked in whispers, '*Whose* baby is that? *Which* Chinaman's?' followed by comments, 'That family is full of *loose* girls. Like wild mother like wild daughter lah. Kahkahkahkah'. At first, it was fine, but it soon became impossible to leave the house without someone saying something about Rahman's skin or eyes. Enough is enough, I said, you can't keep this whole issue to yourself, and Suhana hung her head. Why now? Why now? she asked, as though I were ordering her execution. If not now, then when? When I'm dead and you're old and the boy is a man and wants to know if cancer runs in the family? *Which* family? That's the information he needs. Now, I want the information because I hate the resistance this family is maintaining, as if it's a good thing. She cried and said resisting is hard, it's the pain of a slit between the fingers, not a big cut on the knee. Okay. Sigh. Okay.

When she was about nineteen, she said, she had started seeing a man – a Club man – who was the nicest man a girl could wish to be with. He was tall, thin, rich and yes, he was Chinese. His name was Koh Yee Tai – Koh Yee Tai? I gasped but she treated me like a mere audience – and the thirty-five-year age gap didn't seem at all important because they were in love. He was married with two sons, both a little older than she was. I wanted to tell her, yes, I know all about him. He was the previous year's Club President, the richest man on Coal Island. It had happened on a day when I was busy waitressing and she had gone off to the beach to collect shells. Yee Tai was returning from a swim and she had asked him, 'Isn't it scary to swim in the sea?' He said no and invited her to join him the next time he went. Yee Tai was a sneaky lover, I thought, since when they met at the beach the next day, he took her to a secluded spot, behind a row of coconut trees, rarely peopled due to the rumour that snake nests materialized there like maggots in smelly water. They began their affair which lasted for about six months. It would have continued, she stressed, had his son not found out about it. Sun Lim hated the affair not because it betrayed his mother but because he could not bring himself to believe that his father – in his *fifties* – could entice not just any girl, but a beautiful one, younger than Sun Lim himself. When he raped me, she said, he kept shouting, 'What is it about my father, bitch? What? What? No girl has ever shown even one little bit of interest in me and he, that bloody ageing brute, he gets *you*!' After that Yee Tai and his family disappeared from the Club and Suhana never saw her lover again. But she was left with an eternal token from that period in her life – the son whose father had been the wrong man.

Had it really been a slow drift? Or was it a great gush of water, a waterfall out in the open, not contentedly working in a rainforest, but glaring, bold and unstoppable?

'Rosey! After so long hah! And here you are, still.'

Yes. Working the wheel, polishing the same cups, walking the same grass, nodding at Coach Tan and then spitting into his Screwdriver, smelling Mr Percy Punter's crisp potato wedges, seeing Suhana dive into the pool and surface with shimmering hair and a smooth watery face, wiping shit from babies' bottoms who become men and women, returning to where you'll always be, their mountain, bringing France, Italy, Russia, England, America to you, in fridge magnets. Would they have seen your soul if you dug into your chest and brought it out, a firefly, flickering? It wouldn't matter. They're not there to see your soul, or any soul. They're members who have to eat and play and socialize and let their children eat and play and socialize. What could I ask of them? Nothing.

I went to the Flame of the Forest tree and sat down for a moment. I closed my eyes and heard the sea again. Blankness, like before. I let it be. It was what I had already known. But the blankness moved backward, becoming wallpaper behind the people that now stood, ordinarily. Ibu, Ayah, my sisters, my brother, younger, using more of their limbs, fighting, laughing, preparing for their days, Ayah with his nets, Ibu at her mortar and pestle, the rest with books and bags and marbles. A shadow appeared behind the staircase. I thought I recognized the arms and the tight plait swinging across the banister. The figure moved forward and there I was, holding a *baju kedah* I had stitched before I had known Hisham, before the arrival of the rollercoaster sensations of secondary school love that allow for stones and rocks to be formed and developed and in the end, you have to go to a tree to find answers to mysterious questions.

I opened my eyes and looked up. The flowers were buttons of fire, really orange, really red. I took one of the flowers that had fallen from the tree and then I walked past the club members, past Puna and the others, took my bag of fridge magnets from my locker, gave my key to the receptionist and left. At home, I poured two glasses of water and told Suhana about how I had fallen in love with a boy called Hisham. She cried and I lifted my grandson onto my lap, stroked his head and gave him a raisin bun I had managed to take from the kitchen that day. He had not, after all, been asked to be born the son of a rapist.

6

The Uniqueness of Mynahs

GOD DOES NOT actually live here but I am an old woman and it's better for me to be surrounded by faces other than my own – even if they are made of clay and plaster and only have one expression – than to be forced to contemplate walls, doors, unoccupied surfaces. At dawn the priests ring the bells and bang on the drums, waking up the mynahs and the crows. At dusk the priests ring the bells and bang on the drums, reminding the mynahs and the crows that night is about to come with its floating starlight, floating moonlight. The music of the temple is not pleasant to listen to. It is something to struggle with.

I look up. The mynahs are flying, circling a demon's tongue.

'Come down,' I say, 'come here where you can see everything.' There is a shadow in front of me. It is not mine. It is too wide, too stunted, too crude.

'Bird no come lah,' the shadow says.

'Oh yes they will. You just watch and see. They like to peck at the temple floors', I tell the shadow. I want to turn around to find out what the shadow will finally absorb into.

'So sure hah,' it continues.

The shadow is Chinese. I turn around to confirm its source.

He is shorter than his shadow. He has three or four strands of hair on his head, all long and white but I cannot find out more because he is walking away from me. I follow him to the main shrine where he kneels before it, closes his eyes and mumbles.

'I am Pong Pong,' he says, the final words of his prayer.

'Okay.'

'I go. Tomorrow I coming back.'

I lift my hands and prick my thumb on the cut stone of Krishna's stomach.

I come here because my husband died, because my sons are on the mainland. I break a coconut for them. My sons have met large, dark women with pink red lips. I break coconuts every day and sit on the steps of the temple. That's where the mynahs play. On the pavement layered with old food, animal shit and brown and black and grey spots.

The mynahs fly and land. They are common birds. Their beaks are yellow. They walk like toddlers in diapers. Two mynahs settle their claws on a god's head. They fly off to a shrine but a priest tells them that that is not their place. The mynahs show me that statues can also have big serious eyes.

I sit here, on a temple step, and a mynah drops a twig on my toe.

I sit by Lord Rama at seven in the morning when the sun is a quarter present and sing old Tamil songs from Sivaji Ganesan's films. Sivaji is not just a movie star. There is God in him. *God* put the song and the dance and the words in him. It was Sivaji who brought me and my husband together, brought us together so much that we looked like Sivaji and Padmini, especially in 'Thillana Mohanambal'. Lord Rama anticipates the mornings just as much as I do. Even Sita and Lakshmana, his bodyguards, break out of their statues when I sing 'Marainthirunthu Paarkkum'. My morning ritual is a gathering of gods and mortals, beyond pujas. When I hear a priest's footsteps, I change the lyrics into something more holy.

To be abandoned is chaos.

The garland-maker smiles at me when two mynahs approach my feet.

Pong Pong returns when I sing to Lord Rama. His body is visible to me wherever I look – up, down, this way, that way. He gets up, walks around the temple three times, lies in front of Kali for not enough seconds to make a minute and then he comes to me. He says, 'Very nice lah your voice. What god song this is?'

But I am not going to answer him until he tells me about Kali.

He looks up at Hanuman, in mid-flight on the wall, and is silent for a while. Then he says, 'Aiyah, this one all is private business, Madam. I got my reasons.'

'Okay,' I say, 'then my songs for Rama also private business.'

But he comes back to sit with me. He listens to Sivaji songs, slaps his thighs and twists his head like a drum player.

An oil-lamp wick is being moved about by the wind.

To be abandoned is chaos.

The priests are calm young men. They remind me of my sons, Saha and Aru, both fathers now, both doctors on the mainland. They are not diplomatic like the priests but they have long noses, eyes like plums, chubby chests and legs healthy with hair. Once I said my granddaughter's name, 'Ashoka', and she nodded, but now they say 'How to close the clinic?' That's not the same as not being able to say 'Ashoka' without receiving a nod or a 'Yes, Achi?', I say. But the children have ballet lessons, self-defence lessons, make-your-own-pottery lessons, they say. If they want to see me, they will come.

I stand next to an oil lamp the height of Aru at ten years old. After I sing, Pong Pong and I relocate to the steps of the temple.

I tell the mynahs, 'Pretty, pretty birds'.

'Why you so like them one?' he asks.

'Look carefully lah and you will see.'

'I already look and I don't see anything.'

'Every day they are building things and looking for food. They don't fly as low as swallows. They don't pose like canaries.'

Laughing, he says, 'Next you better go like crow.'

'But,' he continues, 'better not. Got campaign to shoot crow here and if you go like them, you go be sad.'

The gods carry daggers, arrows, pots and forks. They have twins, partners or victims.

By afternoon, a small crowd forms. Some are regulars who come to pray for I don't know what, but they must have very tough lives if they have to see God every day. They kneel down and pull their ears in front of Ganesha, Muruga and Kali. At lunch they open their mouths to eat and talk at the same time. I look for the stone faces. Life is also about chariots, baby demons and giant forks.

Meenachi Muthu likes to interrupt celestial battles.

'Devaki,' she says, 'my daughter is still unmarried. How lah? How lah?'

I smile at my rice and carry on eating. Sometimes I tell her to pray to Durga. When she stops a god from working his bow and that is when I want the arrow to strike, I say, 'Maybe she's meant to be alone.' If she's not talking about her daughter, she's talking about other people's daughters. She should sing Sivaji songs to Lord Rama.

I brush a feather from my lap. To be abandoned is chaos.

I ask Pong Pong, 'How come I never seen you before? Suddenly only you appeared like a ghost or a spirit.'

'Devi, Devi. I always here lah. Just now only you see me.'

'Maybe. Why you come to this temple and not go to the Pagoda?'

'Devi, Devi, don't be like what Malay people say. *Katak di bawah tempurung*. Frog under coconut shell. Can go anywhere to go see God.'

'That means you can go to the Pagoda and see God so why you must come here?'

'Because here got god for everything. When I got no money I go Lakshmi. When I feel stupid I go Saraswathi. When I got enemy I go Kali. I think so if I got constipate also got god I can go see.'

'I see,' I say, thinking about the way he spends most of his time in front of Kali, 'but, you know, you cannot ask God to do bad things for you.'

'Hah,' he snorts, 'Devi, you ah so innocent lah. I know how all this work. My friend before, long time ago, when we work together, he tell me about it.'

'So how come you wait so long to pray?'

'Tut tut tut,' he says, shaking his head, 'I been praying for sixty year lah. But now I want pray where other people got pray. I think so it's more power.'

The temple bells are where birds go to inhale the air, hoping to inhale food.

At the furthest corner of the temple, above a row of angry gods – purple, black, blue and green – are two fierce dragons. They are not Hindu dragons. They are from the Chinese pagoda behind the temple. I sit at the furthest corner of the temple after lunch. The dragons and the gods talk. When it's right, the gods hop onto the dragons and fly into the sky. If I have fish-eyes, I will be able to see not only dragons and gods. To my right, peeping up above Hanuman's head, is the dome of a mosque with a crescent moon on its head like a cherry on a cake. I move from left to right, right to left. On the right, Hanuman flies close to the sun carrying Lanka in his hand. Hanuman meets the gods on the dragons in the sky and they hunt for raksasas. When they return from their adventures, they turn left and rest on the dome, shaded by the crescent moon.

Pong Pong says, 'You go watch mynah lah.'

'I will. I am. There are gods, dragons and one crescent moon.'

'Priest ring the bell.'

'Now look up while the bell is ringing. Catch the gods, the dragons and the crescent moon.'

'It go be good. It good, actually.'

I rub kumkum behind my ears and eat vibuthi.

Meenachi Muthu says to me, 'Oho, Devaki, very nice you have one friend now, isn't it?'

'Oh yes. Friends are always good to have.'

'Acha, acha. Strange he is coming here, no? I mean, these Chinese people cannot let us have the one place that is ours, ah? Why he doesn't go to the Pagoda?'

'Because the Pagoda doesn't have Kali, Parvathi, Lakshmi, Saraswathi, Ganesha, Murugan and Shiva.'

'Of course I know that. But I hear they have pig god and dog god and king god and many more. That's also good what. He belongs there.'

'Why don't you tell him then?'

'Ah, Devaki, but I don't want to ruin things for you.'

'Do whatever you have to lah, Meenachi. Remember, your daughter is still unmarried.'

'Okay, okay, Devaki, no need to be nasty. But I still think these people should know where to go. As if we go and disturb them in their places.'

'Meenachi, sometimes you have to see with fish-eyes.'

I know she will not say more.

Pong Pong and I take the temple steps as our own. We see the pavement, the birds, the chickpea stall, the sun, then the moon, from there.

'Hanuman can fly with dragon also,' he says, 'he one

special monkey. Got God in him one. He go around the world and stop disaster like earthquake and tsunami because he so big can fight earth. Dragon go with him to blow fire at water. Gods sit on his back with magic stick to go put inside the ground to stop earth from shake. But all this not enough. Hanuman is the one who stop disaster in end.'

'Why do you like Hanuman?'

He doesn't reply. He hums, a deep out-of-tune hum of a song I do not know.

Two priests walk by. They smile and disappear. Pong Pong is eighty years old but he looks sixty-eight. I will be sixty-seven later this year. The priests are cooking saffron rice in the kitchen. Pong Pong says he does not want to eat. But he may want saffron rice later, I tell him. The mynahs are disturbing the street sellers.

Pong Pong puts his hand on mine. He says, 'Devi ah. I forget say thank you.'

'For what?'

'You never ask me too much question.'

'Past is past.'

The mynahs land close to us. They peck at the road.

'Ya, of course. But sometime cannot forget some thing.'

'Here I can look at the gods and see what is going on now. And maybe also the future. No one can tell what that is.'

'My future not got much time left. So old already but I feel like I go live eighty year some more. Devi, you know who the person is who tell me about the god?'

The mynahs stop eating and acknowledge each other's existence. They are celebrating something.

'I don't know anything about your past.'

'But you want know or not?'

I look at the birds. They know nothing. They fly and peck and squawk. They lift yellow legs and go everywhere.

I say, 'Well, Pong, if you want to tell then tell lah'.

'Mynah no need get attention to themself. People forgot look at them, forgot they live like all the other bird. They pretty like you say.'

The garland-maker smiles at me when two mynahs approach my feet.

To be abandoned is chaos.

'Who was it who told you about the gods? Mynah bird is it?' I laugh but Pong Pong is staring deep into a mynah's body.

'1948. I inside Communist Party. I want join when Japanese here but my mother say no. Then I become older and go fight get British people out. Don't know how many people I kill. You know live in jungle quite hard. But I really believe to be a Communist. Chin Peng my hero. So brave. I thought in Communist, life got fair but I think so I was young because one day I meet this Indian man in jungle. He work for British. I suppose go kill him but he got beautiful eye and I like him. His name Ganesh, like elephant god. Every day I meet him and he tell me about the different different god. Then I go forget why I join MCP. I only think Ganesh and the god that come save people and how each one go do something special. Ganesh take me to temple and we pray together. I leave MCP and go follow Ganesh. Everything also we do together. Even when Ganesh marry, we do everything together. For sixty year. Last year he die. I stop pray. I go sink in hole. I no want see God. Then two month ago, I dream of him. He say to me, 'Pong, you got go temple again. Pray. Ask Kali kill black demon in your heart.' So I come here lah. I pray but sometime, you know Devi, it not so easy.'

The mynahs have flown away and the crows have stepped in.

'Actually, I think I might also like crows,' I say.

Pong Pong looks at me, undecided about a smile. 'Crow is worser than mynah. Crow common but got no heart and it think it special. Mynah no pretend. It got wing and beak and it just go do what it have to go do.'

Hanuman has joined the gods on the dragon. They hover above the crescent moon on the dome of the mosque, the cherry on the cake. Pong Pong says they are moving westward to kill the ice-demon. When they return Coal Island will be warmer.

Pong Pong and I wipe the gods with wet Kleenex tissues. I say I have sons. He says he's never had children. The tissues turn brown.

I say to him, 'Love, Pong Pong, is like this only.'

7

When Chameleons Migrate

FOR FIVE YEARS the chameleons came out to model on the fence in our garden. When the sun bowed at treetops and the air gave off memories of itself and heat was seen like steam, they leapt out of nature's nooks and began the show. '*Sayang*, they're here,' I would tell Sarimah. She'd come from the kitchen with an empty plate and say, 'Let's pretend we're eating popcorn when we're watching them.' She never introduced other imaginary foods so we ate air-popcorn and waited for the chameleons to turn their heads or to flog their tails against the fence. It was harder to notice exactly when they exchanged their green for orange, orange for brown. Once, a chameleon that seemed more of a jungle lizard swung its neck like a short-put thrower about to make his move. Sarimah's fingers clawed into my arm and I held them, massaging each finger twice while her head moved towards my shoulder. When it landed, her fingers relaxed.

Every March, we brought out the canvas stools that my mother gave us as a wedding present and let the chameleons show off their flow, their comfort in the sun. And then she said, 'We shared all this . . . this life. How could you?'

We met when we were four years old. I don't remember the encounter, but according to our mothers, Sarimah had asked me to say hello to her pet mouse and being unable to find it, I cried and rolled on the floor of the kindergarten classroom saying, 'There is no mouse, there is no mouse.' Sarimah ran around my rolling body screaming, 'My mouse is gone, my mouse is gone.' A teacher settled the dispute with a tin of Hup Seng Assortment Cookies which we returned to every day after that. I do remember searching through the tin for lemon puffs. I suppose our love affair was triggered by a mysterious mouse, nurtured by Hup Seng Assortment Cookies and confirmed by lemon puffs. Then it swelled.

At fifteen, we walked through the neighbourhood just before the sea swigged the sun, when the sky was heavy with purple-pink, pretending to be a roof and then, like a daily surprise, night came and we walked on. She leant her weight on me and I pushed us along the streets, a single egg rolling on flat ground. We stopped when she could see the moon, her favourite item out of days and nights, something she waited for, whether it appeared full-bodied, half-cut or in a slither.

One night, the moon nearly touched Coal Island. The colour of cartoon moons, dirty yellow – reptile eyes in a canopied jungle – it was forcing its way down, having perhaps heard of a thing called gravity. 'A wolf is going to howl any minute now,' I laughed. She removed her weight from my body. 'Fendi, don't say things like that. I'm . . . I'm scared lah. What if it drops? Look at how it has changed colour. It's, it's, it's become evil. I can't stand to look at it,' she said, moving away from where we stood. An owl hooted. A crow shrieked. The moon could not be joked about, I knew that, not in front of her, and I looked back at it, stained with small sweeps of grey. 'Close your eyes,' I said, 'I'm on my way up there. I'm pushing and I'm pushing. It's going up again, Imah. I've got some paint too. I'm painting and I'm painting. Now open your eyes and see.' She walked to where I stood and flung her arms out. 'How you did it, I'll never know,' she said. Her reaching out for the moon, the moon responding by being in its place, the night, the hot smell of magnolias, I, we, were coming out of our hearts. 'We will be married,' I said. She returned to me, gave me her weight and I pushed us back home. There would always be one person for whom I could alter even the moon. But certainties have conditions too.

A life of numbers is what we had. Seventeen years of non-marriage. Five years of marriage. Two months of arguments. Five months of crying. Ten years of kissing. Eight years of lying awake in bed. Twenty-two years of eating. She refused the numbers, wanting only the name that I insisted was other than her, had nothing to do with her. She was complete, a moon of her own. 'She will be the second, always the second to you,' I said. 'The second is the later choice, the one that comes from something the first one can't give and so it is, actually, the first,' she replied, her narrow eyes shutting for a moment. Her dark thin lips, the lips I had always thought of as preserved petals, turned still. 'It is not that,' I said, 'you're not understanding it, Imah. Aishah . . . she's just another part, important, yes, but that doesn't make you less important.' No, she said. Aishah would make her redundant, a lovely thing propped up against a lovely background. She had to be lovely, alone, before a pale, nameless wall, but really, before nothing at all. Now, she wasn't lovely, although yesterday she had plucked white hibiscuses and arranged them in her palms, then crowned herself with them. But Aishah had made the crown, the petals and the stems, unnecessary – a rash construction that came from too much attachment to simple, streaming sunlight, raw mud-smells, and the body of a husband, his arms in the night, his 'good mornings'. No, I said. She was right to make a crown out of the white hibiscuses. She could make another one today, tomorrow, in twenty years and she would still be right. I went to the hibiscus bush, she followed me saying that it was useless, but I continued and plucked the flowers for her. There, I said, take them, please, they are yours, as lovely as the loveliest, you take them, she took them and made a crown but she gathered soil in her hands and crushed it. I wanted to take her to Aishah's apartment to show her that loveliness does not need limitations. But how could I? She had settled in by the crown, garden dirt and insects blending into her *baju kurung*. I needed Aishah's light.

Aishah joined the firm I worked for over two years ago.

On her first day, she stood by the stationery cupboard with her arms crossed over her torso, and a purple handbag in her hands. Her fingernails had been painted orange and yellow, orange on the index finger, yellow on the second one, orange again on the third and so on. Whether she was wearing a dress or a skirt and a blouse was not clear. The blue-green fabric seemed to develop from her body. I had never seen a woman with that much outer complexity, just shining away, strong, convinced of herself, more there than most people. I went to the stationery cupboard not because of her, but my need of a 2B pencil to draw the designs for the new shopping complex the firm was building. That need was left at the desk when I had thought about it, before I had seen the fabric, the nails, the shoes, the handbag, the light in the face, the colour. I did not say hello. Attacked by what I could see, I looked at the cupboard.

'Do you know where I can find Mr Lam Wan Ho?' she said.

Her voice dripped like lonely water in a large, empty room. It was silver, it could shimmer, it was a pendulum, the pendulum at my desk.

'Top floor,' I replied, 'one floor up from here. That's where the directors are.'

'And what do they keep on this floor?' She was a girl, the kind of girl that remained a girl in old age. I only knew of such girls through movies. Yet, here was one.

'Hardworking architects.'

'They need a lot of rulers and shiny straight things, am I right?' She was still open and I suspected that she would never close. It wouldn't bother her to ask, in front of a crowd, what RIP meant, or DOB, for that matter.

'And pencils. That's what I came here for. A 2B pencil.'

'I'll start my work then. Let me get that for you.' She placed the handbag on the floor and the fabric moved along with her body when she knelt.

I didn't tell her where to look even though I knew exactly where she would find a 2B pencil. She was helping, not I.

Her hair, tied in a weak bun, unravelled when she reached for the top shelf of the cupboard. She didn't bother to retie it, tiptoeing further, fingering erasers, rulers, the shiny straight things that architects use which she would find for us, her hair loose and tinted with copper, waves of light brown satin. New, she rolled on, it seemed, away, nonstop.

'I've found a whole box, Mr . . .' she said. Her feet were fully back on the floor.

'Affendi. Call me Fendi, Miss . . .'

'Aishah'. She said her name subtly, like someone who knows a subject so well that they can pick out obscure details that would baffle others.

'Thank you, Aishah,' I said, hoping that I had said her name as she had done. I knew I had failed. It was inevitable.

'You're welcome. Now to find Mr Lam Wan Ho, I just have to go up one floor right?'

'Yes. As soon as you get out of the lift, his office is the second on your left.'

'Thank you.' She walked away, the colour and the light taking off with her and it was a shame to have had all that only to be left with a box of Stabillo 2B pencils.

'You don't look like you're from Coal Island,' I shouted before she could disappear.

'I didn't know it was that obvious!' came the distant reply.

I couldn't help it. I went to the elevator where she was waiting for it and for me too, I wished, and the colour, the voice that dripped like lonely water, the fabric that surged out of her body into soft, undefined patterns became real and wonderful and true when I looked at her.

'Kuala Lumpur. It must be Kuala Lumpur,' I said.

'I have to learn how to look less from there and more from here.'

'No, that would spoil things I think.'

The elevator doors opened. She was stepping in. I could not let them close without something *more*. I would see her in the building again, I knew, but it was this moment that I wanted, the green-blue-orange-yellow-purple atmosphere she had created, the depths of colour and of light.

'Have lunch with me. I can tell you things about the firm. Good for your job,' I said.

'That's nice of you. Okay. Yes. Sure.'

'One at the canteen!'

The elevator doors shut.

At lunch, the women pretended to eat while they watched us with eyes like yoyos. One moment they were up at our faces, the next they were down at our legs. But I kept my legs apart from hers. The men watched us too, struggling, I thought, to fight off her worth, its foundation so secure yet unknowable, like Gaudi's talent.

'Listen,' I said to her, 'if you have lunch with me every day

I promise to teach you what you want to know. About the job. The firm.'

She laughed. She had ruby earrings on and the sunlight made them look like planets of blood.

'You're kind. But do you see the people around us? Are they always this . . .'

'Yes. People here like to come to their own conclusions.'

'And what conclusions would those be?'

'That . . . oh, you know lah!'

She laughed again. 'I don't mind,' she said, 'I'm allowed to have lunch with you.'

She looked at me, skinning me as she did so, all her light assembling in her eyes.

'Yes, I think I will take up your offer,' she said, 'I really don't care about these people but I'm the sort of person who doesn't like people watching me when I'm eating noodles. Rice is okay but not noodles. And you see, the problem is that I love to eat noodles. So what to do? Good news is that my apartment is just up the road. There you can teach me and I can eat noodles in peace.'

I felt the heel of her shoe on my foot.

That day I went home to Sarimah, unstrapped from what I had known or done before, a man who understood that more was coming, that another aspect of himself had emerged, willingly, suddenly. She was sweeping twigs at the entrance of our house when she saw my car and opened the gate, like she always did. 'Imah,' I said, stepping out of the car, 'let's go inside and drink Milo. It's one of those days.' She dropped the broom, ran to me and linked her left leg with mine. It was a thing she did when she wanted to be funny, a gentle, short-lived lady clown. I laughed, I did, because she wanted it and I wanted it too. She was generous after being funny, as if to say, 'Thank you for making me want to make you laugh,' and she'd cook curries, soups, chillied fish, spiced beef and after that, she'd take my stomach in her hands and rub it with Tiger balm, murmuring something like, 'Sleep, sleep, stomach, take away my husband's griefs.'

'Milo hah? Had a good day then? Want to feel warmer hah?' she said, removing her leg from the link.

I wanted to say yes, something sweet and rich and enchanting happened at work today, an event that comes like a sun eclipse, after hundreds of years, which in human life is hundreds of spent emotions and thoughts, and you no longer wait for anything, life is complete, a whole red apple, and you don't think you need to go beyond it and then a moment slides in, exposing not a world of fruits, but maybe of stars, and you have grown.

'It was a good day, Imah,' I replied, 'so good that I want to share it with you.'

'Come, come, Abang, let's go inside and I'll prepare us what you want.'

She enjoyed me in those months, creeping into me, her Husband and her Man, before I could tell her about Aishah. She would not have listened if I said, simply, that I had crossed, in one step, a monsoon drain that I never knew existed. The other side of the drain was not better but it was necessary for the logic of the scene to work. A monsoon drain separates one piece of land. I couldn't explain those things to her, her eyes were still tame, her fingers were still ready to knead my flesh, and she walked with her *baju kurung* grazing the floor. That kind of grace could not take the world without suspicion if something like a monsoon drain-step was mentioned. But I'd have to try with her. I knew. I could not shield my revelation forever.

Of course if Sarimah wanted to be particular, she could have seen herself as a victim when I made that journey to the stationery cupboard and found not only the shady darkness that my 2B pencil would produce but also a breathing merger of colour. But she'd be wrong. A part of my brain had hatched and my heart was reacting, as it had to. If I stopped it, I'd be dishonest, ignoring God's boons, the ones He drops here and there for us to get closer to clarity, to get us closer to Him. Even Sarimah said to me, 'Abang, these days you are more my husband than ever before. You are shining. Some angel must be following you around.' We played, talked, kissed, hugged, talked, but above all, we played. Aishah expanded our marriage, opened up its locked doors and what we found was space, space that goes on and on, bringing together anything at all, and at any time. Sarimah said that the moment had come for us to have a baby.

The day of our wedding was the first time we noticed the chameleons. We were married in the morning when it was mild, soft, moon-like. But as the sun rose and noon approached – the sun finally being the sun it should have been on the island in March – the light became golden orange and heat stepped in for the rest of the day. The tent, set up for the wedding lunch, encouraged humidity to circulate between the hundred or so guests who were already perspiring from the beef curry my *Mak Cik* Su had made and it was hard not to conclude, for me at least, that the weather was conspiring to make her dish less of an attraction. People were using their napkins to wipe their faces and their hands and despite installing extra fans, the heat continued, perpetuating the invention of more immediate fans in the form of invitation cards and wedding money-envelopes. Sarimah said that flies were coming for her and no bride, she rightfully moaned, should have a following of flies to mark her day. I took her to her parents' bedroom where the air-conditioning had sterilized the place, an off-putting prospect for flies. We lay on the bed in silence until she screamed. I grabbed her, waiting to disembowel or behead the beast that had come for my wife. 'At the window . . .' she whispered. Stuck on the window, watching us as though we were actors in a film, was an orange chameleon, something we had never seen before on Coal Island. It didn't look sinister or evil. It was more of a sarcastic creature, eyes half open, thin, stretched lips, an almost-smile, the almost-smile of secretive knowingness. 'It's only a chameleon, *sayang*,' I said. Sarimah, soothed perhaps by the name 'chameleon' or by my voice, or by her own conclusion that our voyeur at the window was just another member of life, laughed and walked up to it. 'It's quite cute,' she said and every March, the month of our wedding and of the chameleon parade, she'd say, 'So cute'. I discovered from *Pak Cik* Nizam that the year we got married was also the first year of chameleon migration from the mainland to Coal Island.

I never thought of *replacing* Sarimah with Aishah. They were two women with two ways of breathing, of touching, of walking, of speaking. Aishah would say, 'Criss-cross my heart with your hands. Now, do it, now. You are the only star in my sky,' and then she would jump up as though she were reaching for a light bulb before diving onto me. Her fingers, long, narrowing at the tips, spotlighted everything they touched. A chipped vase was beautiful because it was chipped when Aishah's finger landed on it. 'Of course a man like you already has someone to love,' she said to me not long after we met, 'That's why I feel special. You don't need me. You want me.'

'No,' I replied, 'not quite right. I need you as much as I need Imah. It's a . . . strange situation to be in. It's like this. You are happy, then you find out that you can be happier. Not just that you can, actually, it's more like you *must*.'

She didn't know what I meant, she said. In any case, she was happy to contribute to my happier happiness. But, I responded a while later, it's not even happiness, it's something else, a thing with no name. A finger, one of those fingers that changed whatever it touched, stroked one of mine.

Sarimah's fingers were small, all of similar height, the thumb and the first finger closer to identical twins than to egg-selfish siblings. They could bend backward and forward, jostle amongst themselves, and if ever the magical moment came when they could be detached from her hands, I'm quite sure, they would be acrobats, swinging east to west and back again. Those fingers settled on chair-backs, the lightly embroidered ones that she loved collecting which also manipulated how our sofas looked. Her fingers fit into my hand at night, a way for her to be guided in her dreams. 'We are walkers, you see,' she once said, 'we love to walk so even in sleep we walk, my hand in yours, even though we're elsewhere.' She was not my shadow, but my organs, I told her, and Aishah my blood; a system that works for pure life.

'No, no,' she said when I finally explained my revelation, 'what do you mean by two wholes making a whole? It makes no sense. No sense at all.'

There are crude ways of explaining how love does not go through a funnel, directed by an instrument, contained in a tool. Sarimah would not have wanted such an analogy, anyway. She wanted clean answers, literal, scientific, easy to digest.

'Aishah will be my second wife,' I said, hating those words, preferring to have told her about love, the funnel, the freedom.

She didn't respond right away. She looked at me with nothing on her face, hoping to find, I thought, something on mine. Unsatisfied, she said, 'Only *something* like you can do a thing like *this*!'

'It's not a thing, Imah. It's real, it lives.'

She grabbed a chair-back and threw it in my direction but it barely reached me.

'Imah, listen, please. I'm not committing a crime. It *can* be ordinary. It *is* legal. Don't make me seem like a criminal.'

She tried again with another chair-back but received the same result. 'Of course you are a criminal! There are many kinds, you know. Don't you know? Crimes against love, that's what.'

'What about the Prophet's wives? Didn't they share him? They knew no possession. Isn't that love? What crime is that?'

'You can bring up history, Bang, but it's no use,' she said, her voice soft, sounding like it wanted to end, 'it's people who matter. The ones in front of your eyes.'

'What are you saying?'

'I'm saying no. I won't agree. You won't take a second wife.'

There were no expansive philosophies on love that she would allow me to give her. Some animals, I told her, share each other, giving, always giving, they become one collective soul. But she wanted the past, the kindergarten friendship, the teenage night-walks, the hot wedding day, the chameleons. I could almost imagine her thinking, 'And now I'll be alone, rejected, lost in my own house.' How could I tell her, no, that's not true, you're here, a Proper Person, a Loved One, my Lover, my Very First Wife?

Then, one day, coming out of the shower, she said that the baby in her stomach would be fatherless, a worse thing, I decided, than me failing to convince her that she was a Proper Person, a Loved One, my Lover, my Very First Wife.

'Imah, *sayang*,' I said, 'it is ours, that life there, we made it, half and half, it will always be a bit of me and a bit of you.'

'Yes,' she replied, 'that is how God wanted it to be. A marriage is a bit of man and a bit of woman. Not one bit man and two bits woman.'

It was the baby – the one that hid in her stomach, known only to her, feeling it as I would never be able to until it came out of hiding – that changed the problem. Could something I created be unknown to me, forever? When it grew up, would it look at me and see nothing? A pale stranger, just another hand held out for a shake, a man with a beard and lines on his face, smiling, an idiot. Would that be what it saw in the future when I followed it around town, waiting to start a friendship, a relationship, anything? Is that what the love that does not go through a funnel does?

I begged Sarimah to let me get close to her belly. Let me touch it, feel it, the baby, I said, you've said no to the marriage, so I won't, I *can't*, let me touch it, feel it, the baby.

But she said, 'What's done is done. I wasn't enough. You had the intention. That's all I need, to know what you think of this marriage. Leave us alone. That's the best gift you can give this baby.' I held on to her legs, her arms, her feet, pleading, crying, let me have the baby too, I said, but she looked at me as though I wasn't there, a piece of air that blends in with the rest of the atmosphere.

'Imah, don't you see?' I said, 'I love you!'

'Go,' she replied.

I packed my suitcase feeling boneless, light, unnecessary. I walked out and the chameleons were on the fence, at least five of them and all at once, they looked at me with their half-open eyes, as if to say, 'What a life, hah?' Then I heard the snickering. Keh keh keh, went the chameleons, their tongues stretched far out of their mouths, their skin making a rare impulsive switch from orange to green. I went to Aishah's apartment and she said as she took my things in, 'So now we can be together, yes?' I didn't, couldn't respond.

They were supposed to be as they had been, my days with

Aishah, full of movement and colour and light and they were, to some degree, but my body had snapped, some bone or vein had clicked and left an excess of space, of displaced blood.

'It's easy,' Aishah said, her eyes still glittering, still settling into my body, 'all you have to do is divorce her since she won't agree to you taking a second wife'.

'That's actually the difficult part. I don't want to divorce her. I need her. I need you. If it's one or the other, then I should be alone.'

'That's so silly lah. Sometimes you have to choose. Some women are okay with sharing, others, not really. At the end of the day, Fendi, you have to respect what she wants.'

'You and Sarimah, you both don't understand. It's about the question of balance. What is the world? It's made up of many, many pieces and we need those pieces, all of them, to be ourselves.'

'You're talking dangerously. Why can't you just accept that you're with me now?'

'I'm here am I not?'

She agreed but after that she went to the bedroom and began reading a magazine, ignoring my questions about what she wanted for lunch or if she needed a drink.

I left the apartment, wondering if I should visit Sarimah but I knew that she wouldn't want me so I went to Halim's house, an old friend, a man who had two wives.

'You look so pale lah these days,' he said, handing me a cup of tea that one of his wives had prepared. Zainor and Sharifah had agreed to live in one house provided that they each had a room of their own.

'Woman problems,' I tried to laugh. The tea scalded my tongue. I wondered which wife had done that to me.

'That one will always be there lah. Where got life without a woman breaking your heart or telling you that you must change? What's wrong with Sarimah? Or is it that woman I heard you've been mixing with?'

Zainor walked in just as I was about to reply. She was a plain woman whose plump face seemed to project out of her head scarf which was tied so tightly that it was a wonder she could breathe. She didn't smile when she said hello.

'Nor, make sure Ipah has cleaned out the second bathroom. We had a bit of an accident last night. I hope we didn't wake you,' Halim said. Zainor nodded and left as quickly as she had come in.

'It doesn't bother Zainor?' I asked, thinking for the first time about the practicalities if Sarimah and Aishah agreed to live together. Sarimah would have me the most. Aishah and I would talk and touch when Sarimah was bathing or praying or attending to the baby. I missed them together, a ridiculous thing to miss, I knew, since I had never had them.

'No lah. How many years we've been living like this already? There's a system.'

'I wanted to take a second wife but Sarimah couldn't accept it. She asked me to leave. How come it's so easy for you?'

'Ah, well, not all women can take it. My women . . . they work so well together. You just have to be lucky to find the right combination. Also, remember what the Quran says, marry women of your own choice, up to four, but if you can't deal with them *justly*, then you cannot marry them all. Understand? *If* the women cannot agree with each other, then at some point, you will be unfair. Zainor and Ipah . . . they're sisters.'

When I was leaving Halim's house I saw Zainor in the hallway. She nodded and I nodded back. Her flat cheeks suggested that she was morose but above that her eyebrows tilted, and she came off looking peaceful, like a grown woman asleep. I could not think of anything to say and so I left, without words.

Every day, Aishah said that we had to be married and my repeated response was that I didn't understand her. But she insisted, 'We can't go on living like this.' I said I was struggling and that I was dreaming of Sarimah and the baby and divorce was such a big word. But she carried on, 'Please, Fendi. You love me so what's wrong?' I needed to maintain the balance or lose it completely, I wanted to say, but she had already refused that reasoning. Then one day she said, finally revealing why her desperation was so severe and confusing, 'You don't understand. It's a serious thing . . . what I've been given. I just want to marry you. I'm dying.' She'd been born with a condition, something to do with an absence of blood cells and the doctors had given her till the age of twenty four to live. 'But you're twenty five,' I said. 'So you see now, don't you? I've overshot the limit,' she replied. It was hard to believe that she could die, not that Colour, not the woman with light and a voice like gorgeous metal, like lonely water dripping in a large, empty room. All that flesh and paint and movement to just end? It didn't seem appropriate for her.

The decline, at first, was slow. Her skin, from oiled bronze became stained copper, and her arms twitched but she could still speak and laugh. When she couldn't walk, I checked her into the hospital where she remained till the end. I did try for her, to see if I could give her what she wanted. I visited Sarimah when she was six months pregnant with our child. She was sitting in the garden with a cup of ginger tea, watching the chameleons.

'They're out again,' I said, 'it's September. They shouldn't be.'

'Yes, well, things change, you know,' Sarimah replied. I nodded and sat down next to her.

'Remember the first time we saw them?' I asked.

'The day we got married. I thought to myself then that they brought good luck. I think differently now.'

'What do you mean?'

'As I said, things change.'

'They do. Aishah . . . she . . . she's not well, Imah. Not long left. She's sick at home but I think soon she'll have to go to the hospital. She wants me to marry her. Please, Imah. It's her dying wish. You will never have to live with her. You'll have me back. Just . . . allow us to marry.'

She got up and went to the chameleons. 'You see them? They may change colour but they have become a constant.' She returned to the house and locked the door behind her.

After Aishah's funeral I gathered her things and paid for a delivery service to take them to Kuala Lumpur. She had left the apartment to me. I said to myself, 'Well, now, this is where I'll be.' I put up paintings of birds and horses, bought vases and filled them with wildflowers, stacked coasters on the kitchen table and gave away the television. In the evenings, I sat by the window; looking at the close or distant moon, thinking about its surface, whether it was rough, smooth, stony or grainy. I got nowhere, of course, but each night the moon was a different place, charmed, wild, drawing me in and I could know no better. It was like flipping the pages of a single book for the rest of my life. I did think about Sarimah and the baby and yes, I knew, they were still a part of me as was Aishah's ghost that sometimes appeared in the sky. But now there was also the moon, the single book and its pages.

A year after I left my home with Sarimah, she appeared at my apartment. The baby, a girl, was bigger than a baby.

'Fendi,' she said, 'the chameleons, they're gone'.

'But it's March.'

'I suppose, like I said before, things are changing or have changed, I don't know. Can't depend even on the chameleons. Fendi . . . I . . . will you come home?'

I looked into her eyes. They were not the same as they had been before. Something light and grey had entered them. The baby stared at me and held out a hand. I touched it, feeling the rubbery softness of new life. It had already become strange to me, stranger than when it had hidden out in Sarimah's stomach.

'This is the second life I said I have. If you can accept it then I'll spend half my days with you.'

She took the baby's hand away from mine. 'When will I ever learn that I can never be *it* for you?'

She left and never returned. Later I found out that chameleons migrate because they seek a place that can give them what they need – more sun, more heat, more fences to parade on. Far away, on another island perhaps, my chameleons are twisting and changing for a couple who can never know what the years will do to them.

8

My Tapir, My Peril

30/8/2009

Dear Papa,

I'm sorry. You'd want another letter in the postbox: the bank telling you that you've won a car, *Reader's Digest* announcing that you're one step away from becoming a millionaire, Auntie Sue confessing why she hasn't spoken to you since Ma's death. Those are the letters that you hope will come; you don't think about them, they are already in you, unlike this letter. You'll see the Selangor stamp and not worry about what's inside until you start reading and a close life, started and ended years ago, returns to you, out of these sheets that I tore from the Dear Diary you gave me when I was ten and could never write in. This is no Dear Diary, Pa. I am beyond writing in private and for privacy, stuffing the soul with ideas that eat the lonely hours and grow fat because nobody's looking at them. This is one mind seeking out another. You may stop reading but that would be wrong. Any kind of search should never be stopped. Let's be philosophical about this, Pa, I mean *come on!*

If I'm not too late, don't put this letter down. Not until you think of our green-tiled roof, Bobo's chewed slipper, your pitcher of cola on the hall table during the monsoon season, the frangipanis in the garden. These are the things that move through our lives, the ones that don't jump out but silently appear as if somebody's playing a slide show, projecting the visions onto places that are far away from where they were first formed. You must see them too, one fragment at a time, appearing before sleep, an image that brings out every word, action and thought of the past and the future. You realize that you were born. (You are free to conclude that your little daughter has grown up! Seriously though, Pa, how else could you approach this letter?)

When it happened (or at least when I found out) I went to the fringe of the jungle. I know you told me never to go there but the moon was so bright and it didn't even seem that it was nighttime or that I had to look out for toads, snakes, leaping frogs, you know, the stuff of slime! I wanted to sit and watch how the leaves touched one another. I wanted the darkness of the bushes and the invisible crickets and owls. You always said the jungle was for no one except for the life already in there. But I needed such a place to surprise me, to have, for example, a leopard walk out, see me, and walk back in, or, even better, to chill out at my feet. Something like warmth could come from the jungle. It had to. How can you say you know your body when it begins to turn differently, and jiggle at new places, and produce what seems too bizarre, yet too familiar? A seed, Papa! A whole seed inside me! Or at least, a person the size of a star anise. Suddenly life had doubled up. I was life, then more than life; cheetahs, tigers, panthers, leopards, gathered in me, filled into a single star anise, a spice that floats through curries, giving flavour until it is discovered and it becomes a mystery, its juices too strong.

I didn't go into the jungle. I sat before it, watching and listening, pressing my hand against my stomach and moving it around. If I heard a pop, I'd have got it, and I kept doing it, waiting for the massage to give me what I thought I wanted but an animal screamed and I ran away from the darkness and from the scream that I knew had to be an animal's but couldn't have been because it wasn't in any animal's vocabulary. Strange, Papa. I was running away from you too.

I went to the playground. The moon was still as bright as ever; I lay down on the slide and closed my eyes. You emerged, poofed out, and returned with your head coming out of the baby's neck; Hui Ling appeared, holding Bobo, and behind them Ponniah was waving. I opened my eyes and the characters vanished. I closed my eyes again and they had changed roles, more outrageous this time, you having even developed a tail! I sat up to adjust my position and there it stood in the moonlight like one of the characters I had just banished but my eyes were open. It was large, heavy and very still, a buffalo or a hormone-injected pig, I thought, but I squinted and it was not so. Standing in our local playground where children go to lose themselves was a tapir. A tapir,

Papa! I couldn't believe it. I quietly got off the slide but before I could take my first step, it was gone. Too abruptly, I thought. Perhaps it wasn't a tapir. It might have leapt out of my closed eyes and tried to live in the waking world but it couldn't and so it dissolved like heated sugar. What if it was a tapir? It followed me from the jungle and enjoyed watching me as I enjoyed watching the darkness of the jungle until something real surfaced – a scream, a girl's movement – and the event goes bust.

When I got home you were asleep and forgetting that I was avoiding you, I sat in the hall, the lights off, in danger of, yet oblivious to the possibility of your creaking down the stairs for a glass of water. The tapir had stood there, I thought, maybe. Could the mind create big objects and transfer them, for a second or a millisecond, to actual sight, or was it actual space? I did not know the answer; a teenage girl is not supposed to be that aware or that inclined to ask questions about the mind, the imagination, reality, correct or no, Papa?

But you see, I think any girl who walks into Dr Singham's clinic will ask different – higher – questions than girls who don't. That's the nature of the thing, the surprise star anise; it makes you *think*, like when you assume you're healthy and a blood test tells you otherwise. Suddenly, you wonder if the way you had been cooking your rice was wrong, or if you had washed spoons correctly, chewed enough times before swallowing, cleaned your toes with cotton buds and Dettol. Wasn't that how Ma behaved? How quickly she died. And then people came to the house bringing Nyonya curry, fried rice, cakes, pears, oranges, soup; Kevin Pillai's mother (you know, the one with the mad daughter) saying to me, 'Hui Yong, your Papa is the bravest man we know lah. Lost his wife and then he has to take care of two young girls. You better help your Papa, okay, girl?' It was nice to be seen by everybody. I was the strong, grieving first daughter, still young at seventeen but already old; Hui Yong was the second daughter, silent, too young to understand what Ma's passing had meant. And you were simply the widower, too handsome for that role – your hair styled and black – a man made more to drive a Range Rover around the hills of the island than to have a dead wife and two living daughters. Is that why our visitors were mainly morning-marketing housewives? You liked the deboned fish they brought you, I could tell, because you swept your hair from forehead to head. Ma said you did that to indicate 'suave joy'. You had style, she said, and you showed your visitors a lot of style; they didn't care that their legs of lamb or chicken livers were being eyed by Bobo. And as I watched you in the kitchen, I felt something unknown to me. I was inside myself and that inside was so big, Papa, so *wild* that I didn't know what to do with it, the 'it' being what was unknown to me which could fly everywhere but only inside me. Maybe it was the way you didn't know I was waiting at the kitchen door that created 'it'. I don't know. Anyway, I digress. That's what happens when there's too much to tell. I was talking about the tapir.

I didn't go looking for it after that moonlit night at the playground. When morning came the next day, I was back at my body, checking my stomach, pressing it, trying to feel the star anise shift or breathe. Then I thought that maybe it wasn't there and that the tapir had never appeared. I'd have said to you if Ma were alive, 'Pa, I saw the most ridiculous thing the other day. A tapir stood in the playground as if it really belonged there.' But I couldn't, you see. You'd react, and then we'd have silence because you'd be waiting for me to say something else and we'd end up talking about what we could have for dinner. I had become a woman at the age of eighteen! Don't forget, that was the day I had found out about the star anise and I kept thinking that even if I sucked it out of my womb, its ghost would remain inside me forever and if I ever had another child, it would slide into the next star anise and haunt its sibling, again, forever. Papa, you weren't the only one suffering. In fact, I would say, I suffered more. You only had the *knowledge* of what was happening. I was *living* it. To be very honest with you, I didn't care that the people on Coal Island knew the whole story. I just regret that they found out before you did and that you had to hear about it from one of the morning-marketing housewives.

Papa, remember when you, Ma, Hui Ling and I used to sit in the garden and stare at the roof? You said that when the house was built Ma wanted green tiles on the roof, not the regular red ones; emerald stones over our heads, she said when she was pregnant with me, let this baby have a bit of enchantment, and not just from Snow White and the Ice Queen, no, the baby will turn her head up and see jewels, her parents' jewels, for her. I tried hard to find the stones but it was always Hui Ling who screamed, 'I found twenty jewels!'

How was I to know that the whole thing wasn't real and that I had to imagine it was? The green-tiled roof, our own, shining in the sun like greasy peas. Privately, I wished I could've had Ma's kind of faith that billowed, a flag on a windy day, moving like mad but still in place. Genes are funny, isn't it? You get some and then the rest are turned around. After Ma died, I carried on seeing green tiles, not emeralds. But that's okay. You can't change sight and you can't force sensations onto yourself. The frangipanis, though, were mine, the flowers of death according to the Malays, and even if they were, I didn't mind. The frangipanis startled, whispered, fought evil, in our own backyard. That was the greatest. What I'm trying to say is that when it rains hard and the wind outside is wild, I drink cola from a pitcher with a circle of daisies around the rim.

I saw the tapir again a few days later, without searching for or even expecting it. It was real; that's right I said to myself, It. Is. Real. The moon was not as bright as it had been on the night of the first sighting but it was luminous enough to sit in the playground and still be able to see the outline of objects. I was asking myself what I found in that blah playground when it surfaced in the same spot as before. I got off the slide, stretching my legs like a thief, and told the tapir, 'I'm only Hui Yong. I'm only Hui Yong.' I stood a few metres apart from it, close enough to see its black-and-white fur, how it carried opposites on its body, sewing a landscape so exact that the two would never clash. We remained like that for a few minutes, me staring at it and it looking ahead of itself, as if only it existed. Then it turned around and walked away, god knows where. I mean, tapirs are endangered. They don't have the luxury of returning *anywhere*. Could it really – having come from nowhere – have survived alone somewhere, amidst overflowing leaves and shoots and vines and thorns, wandering residential areas for exercise? A stray cat could have done that, a stray dog, certainly, especially if it was a member of a pack and wanted to be free, solitary, for a moment in the night when the rest were howling at the moon and it preferred not to. So where was my tapir going? But it was too dark, Papa, and what if it wasn't a part of the world? That's what I thought then, crazy, I know, since I saw it and I don't believe in magic. Yet it had magic inside all that blood, flesh, vein and bone. But I had to let it go back to where it came from – a bend in the jungle, perhaps a place I had never seen – because, let's face it, what would I do with it anyway? Now that I think back, it was only the darkness that stopped me from following it. If the night had been brighter, I'd have gone with it. Its fatness told me that it was real, ordinary, simply an animal. Its colouring suggested it was not all animal. It was a black-and-white toy, better than a zebra because the zebra could only commit to one shade for a short time before giving in again to the other. You see, Papa, the tapir was fully up and down, heaven and hell, woman and man!

I think before I carry on with the tapir, it's the right time to bring up Ponniah, my gold-toothed interruption of days passed in your house – no longer sitting on the patio to discuss the roof or when flower buds bloomed – but in a corner with a piece of fruit and a magazine while you were in the kitchen, entertaining, taking impromptu cooking lessons and Hui Ling trapped flies or spiders wherever there was rot, cobwebs. Those days, months after Ma had defied the doctors and died half a year before she was meant to, were contradictions, don't you think? They were happening, minute by minute, and in that sense, definitely progressing – 1 p.m., 2 p.m., 3 p.m. . . . midnight) but I never felt them move. It's as though they were dead, like her; we lived in dead hours, yet you talked and made your first ever upside-down pineapple cake. I ate it in secret behind the college bicycle shed on the same day I tripped on a stone in front of a construction site. A dark, wet-looking Indian man, held out a hand and said, 'Got be careful, girl. This kind of place all not for chirren'. Normally, for me, he would have been a thug since he had a fat stomach, tight skin, a smile that wasn't a smile and he wore earrings. But he continued to speak. 'Why you walk your own? Not safe. People watch and can do bad thing to you. I okay. I got no problem with you. Other people I got problem with.' Then he offered me a cup of tea from his flask and I took it although I didn't need tea. I wasn't injured. I'd never spoken to a construction worker before. Why hadn't I? He was talking freely. I was just another person to him. He had deep eyes.

'Who do you have a problem with?' I asked. He looked at me, grinning in the way that people do when they're not actually entertained but annoyed.

He didn't answer. He seemed to be thinking about things that did not belong to a construction site like what happens in the sun, maybe, or the reason we are here – huge, painful grown-up issues that are hardly considered although they really should be but people prefer to talk about the price of petrol. Like how we talked about furniture when Ma had cancer.

'This country,' he finally said. He was looking out at nothing. It's the look of beholding hills, the sea, wide fields, not unlike my tapir's look, now that I think back. And until today I don't know why he opened up to me like that.

'I don't understand.' The tea was undrinkable. I tasted condensed milk, powdered milk, half a bag of sugar, maybe even honey, and then tea, a dust of tea.

'Ai . . . you don't see, ah? What you but young girl eh? Thing is this. They treat me like one pariah. I got no right is it? If God make me Chinee or Malai, okay I say, okay. But now no meaning. Tomorrow is what? *Merdeka*! Chik! (and then he spat) What got free here?'

What was he saying? I wanted to know. Then in a soft voice he spoke.

His family once lived on a rubber estate on the island which was cleared for the building of the Syok! Shopping complex. The ten families that lived there were not notified that their homes were going to be torn down. The bulldozers arrived one day and the destruction began. There was no opportunity for the families to even protest or at least debate it out with the authorities. They were given money to start their new lives elsewhere. But people can't be asked to begin again when they haven't had the chance to mourn for what they had lost. Their lives and memories, he said, ended up in the ruins of their old homes. Ponniah's family moved to a low cost flat and were miserable there. They were poor, very poor, since his mother and his sister didn't work as one was too old and the other disabled. Their sole breadwinner, he only earned RM 500 a month. He couldn't afford a lawyer and no one would listen to him. He wrote many letters in broken Bahasa (maybe that's why they couldn't take him seriously). 'But I nobody,' he said.

What do you do when someone tells you that?

I hugged him.

He recoiled, at first. 'Never think you will do that,' he said once he touched my hips.

I understood what it was like to live with no hope. If something as big as a country paves that road for you, it's worse, more significant than a personal circumstance that freezes hope for a while before the thaw comes, years later, when a person or an event does it for you. His hopelessness became my hope and for him, perhaps, I was the hope to his hopelessness. Can you see how such things happen, Papa?

We met the next day. *Merdeka.* The day Malaya became free.

Tanggal tiga puluh satu . . .

Bulan lapan lima puluh tujuh

. . . Merdeka, Merdeka . . .

Flags everywhere, stuck on cars, hung on the windows of government buildings, corporate buildings, flats, bungalows. The TV played *Merdeka* songs and the parade was on. In between those broadcasts was Tunku Abdul Rahman standing with a straight back, holding his hand up and shouting the words of freedom in that old-time voice.

Ponniah said, 'You free only if you success fighting to

free.' That was true, I thought. What does it mean to be free? Isn't freedom different for different people?

Ponniah and I spent the whole of *Merdeka* together. I'm not sure what you were doing but I do remember telling you that I was with Daisy D'Cruz and you seemed to listen although I wasn't sure that you had. We sat at the construction site, just us two, since the workers were off on that day. He brought out his flask and I didn't know what I would say if he offered me a cup of tea again. Thankfully, it was toddy. It was sweet, a little musty, but generally sweet and I liked it. I drank cup after cup, wanting more, until I couldn't stand up and he sat me against the wall. 'Drink water, girl,' he said and I did. His arm on mine made my dizziness fiercer and I pulled him towards me, for a hug, and then it happened. It was my first time, Papa, I swear. Difficult, painful, weird, yes all those things, but also, familiar, warm, right. When it was over I saw his body sagging, less than tight, his belly great and heaving, the opposite of his body with clothes on. I ran.

I ran with no destination in mind. His chest had been like tough meat, stinking and hard. His hands were claws. His feet were webbed. His pull was preying. When had I seen the man in him? I felt dirty for thinking of him like that, dirtier than having let myself touch him.

How was I to know that I was so unlucky? That my first time would lead to the biggest taboo of all?

I only visited Ponniah after I found out, after I had seen my tapir, and you know what he did? He laughed. Yes, Papa, he laughed right into my face and said, 'Not my problem.' Then he continued piling bricks.

I went to the fringe of the jungle and then to the playground which was where, as you know, the tapir appeared.

I mentioned earlier that I had decided to follow the tapir the next time I saw it and I did. It was about a week after the last sighting. I admit I did go back to the playground every night to see if it was there. I'd lie still on the slide with my eyes open, hoping to catch it. When it finally came I did what I did before. I walked quietly up to it and looked at it while it ignored me. But I could tell that it knew I was there and liked me being there. Oh, Papa, it was my new friend! ('He', by the way, and not 'it'. I named him Peril because, you know, he's endangered. Okay, okay, I know that peril technically means danger, but what kind of a name is Peril anyway?) When he started to move, I brought out my torch just in case. He walked slowly so it was easy to follow him. He was like a fat auntie who'd just had a big brunch. We ended up at an abandoned house. Peril entered it as if he owned the house. Then I heard a voice. I hid behind a bush and waited. 'Blaardy basterd! Blaardy hanimal!' It was Ponniah. Ponniah, Papa, Ponniah! I saw him grab Peril and tie him to a pillar. I had so many questions. I mean, what was Ponniah doing with Peril and why was he being loud, rude and harsh? When he hit Peril, I got up, banged the gate open and faced Ponniah. 'What do you think you're doing?' I said. I must say, Ponniah was so shocked to see me that he went from dark to light brown. It wasn't just Peril who was inhabiting the abandoned house. There was also a marbled cat and a cheetah. Don't ask me how he managed to capture them. It must be because he's an animal himself.

So, he had gone beyond his RM 500, I thought. Easily. Who knew how long and to what extent his wildlife zoo had been in operation.

I had told him, days before, when I was suddenly brave to talk about the star anise, 'Mr Ponniah –' and he butted in, 'No, girl. You learn nothing ah after that day? Call me Uncle.'

'Uncle,' I said, 'I've been sick.'

'You go see doctor lah,' he replied, flattening a glob of cement on a brick.

'Already, Uncle, already seen.'

'Good, good. You go back now to house. I got work.'

'But . . . I'm, you, we, I am pregnant, Uncle.'

He turned around. There were two thick veins conjoining above his eyebrows. 'Who the blaardy basterd?' he whispered.

And I whispered back, 'You.'

I admit, Pa, he didn't laugh. I said he laughed to make the writing easier.

He said, Oh, this is hard! He said, 'You live with me. My Amma help with baby.'

Live with him? 'No,' I replied, 'I'm eighteen. I have a family. I can't live in a flat with you, your mother and your sister.'

I could only think of me sitting on a balcony that had never been swept, hearing a child cry and two women singing strange lullabies.

'The baby always mine,' he said and I ran, my favourite way of escaping Ponniah.

But there, in that house of captives, I could not run. I

demanded that he release the three captives. Of course, he wasn't going to listen to me. He was a big man, Papa. What could I do? The way Peril looked at me then is impossible to describe. I was helpless. Totally. I thought that if Ponniah wasn't there, then the animals could go back to the jungle and be who they had to be. Okay, so here's what happened. Papa, please, don't judge. I did what I had to do to save our Malaysian wildlife. When Ponniah was busy kicking Peril, I hit him with my torch. He fell unconscious and I went on to strangle him with my hands. My hands, Papa! He died. I released Peril and his friends and when I got home that night I told you I was pregnant because I knew you'd hate me and that would be the best reason to leave. But of course, with this being Coal Island, you had found out earlier that day that I had gone into Dr Singham's clinic. You were just waiting for my confirmation. I know. I went to see if my body could take an abortion. Or rather, whether my mind and heart could.

Ponniah shouldn't have deprived us of what wanders about our jungles. Look, there's a reason Peril's called a *Malayan* Tapir. It's here, ours, a chance to love, the last of our hope. I loved Peril. He shouldn't have done that.

Let's just say, Papa, that I'm a very human human being. When I arrived in Kuala Lumpur, I found a retail job and have been there ever since. The star anise, I decided, would become a full grown star. That's right, Papa, you have a granddaughter. She'll be three tomorrow. *Merdeka* day. I've called her Mei Chyn, after Ma. The first year was the most difficult period in my life. I had what they call post-natal depression and basically, I came out of that triumphant. It's the tapir, Papa. Peril showed me how the black and the white have to be themselves and that Ponniah was just following that pattern of in and out, yes and no. You see how it works? It'll always be like this. Question is how do you carry them on one body, like Peril? Well, I've come up with a theory. You go along until you become as desperate as Ponniah. But at some point, you have to let the revelations come.

Ponniah or Peril? There's a fine line between the perilous and those in peril.

So there we are, Papa. That's what happened to me. By the way, it's *Merdeka* tomorrow and Mei Chyn and I are celebrating her coming-into-this-world with a good old toast to Prime Minister Tunku. He pronounced those words of freedom which I've abided by all these years. I did, after all, save the tapir. When I know the letter's reached you, we'll be making a trip to Coal Island. Come on, you don't want me to forget my roots, do you?

Lots of love,
Hui Yong and Mei Chyn xxxx

9

Catching Iguanas

WHAT PEOPLE DIDN'T understand about me was that I returned only because I had no choice. They saluted me for coming back to the island when my thoughts were with my local pub and Gemma and our half-heated flat on Parkview Avenue. It's been five months since my visa expired. In the first few weeks I sat in bed, turning the pages of my passport, touching the stamps of entry, imagining the smell of icicles and of clothes drying on radiator tops. Slowly Gemma's hand would enter the picture, a slim white hand adorned with beaded bracelets and sapphire bangles, moving to collect papers or to soak a tea bag in a painted mug of boiling water. After the hand came the shoulders, skeletal and freckled, looking as though they would snap if they were touched. Then her whole form would appear in front of me, like a sculpture. The hands, once flitting from papers to mugs to incense burners, stiffened. The eyes, green globes of stone, implied apology. She did not speak. More recently, she has disappeared altogether. Even her photographs no longer bring back her hologram. And she has stopped writing.

Over three years ago Coal Island turned monochrome, every wall and tree, a variation of the colour brown. I moved between one friend, a set of parents and a sister who had just been diagnosed with manic depression and was therefore more important than I was.

I said to my friend Kumar – who was also indirectly dismissed in his household, in his case, for being a writer – when we were drinking Jumbo Juice at a *mamak* stall one evening, 'You ever think it'd be nice to leave this place?'

'Leave?' he replied, looking shocked, 'never, man. This island is bursting with stories.'

'That's good for a writer but what am I to do with stories? Damn it lah, my *life* is one of those stories. You know what it's like to live with a mother who keeps telling her daughter 'Come on lah, Mary darling, Mummy's own special child, just eat one spoonful. Then you can go back to bed. Mummy promise, okay?'And you know what that's for? Just to make her eat four spoonfuls of porridge. Then she'll talk all night. On and on she goes. Suddenly, she'll stop and my mother cries in the toilet. She thinks I can't hear her? And my father is patting Mary on the head, saying, 'It's okay, molé, just one word. I know you can do it.' Go on. Take my life and write your story. But I tell you what, there's no way I'm staying here much longer. And you want to know something else? When I leave, my parents will feel better because then they can really live together, just the three of them.'

'So what's the plan?'

'I've applied for a scholarship. England, Kumar, England. When I get there, I'm never coming back.'

'Take care, Kevin. No one should try to forget that much. You'll come back for visits.'

'No way. Once I'm gone, I'm gone.'

It took the family nineteen years to realize that Mary was not just volatile. All the while, Mary's tantrums were simply Mary's tantrums. Once, she stared at a garden-plucked leaf for days, saying nothing to us and then she announced, 'I'm going to become a biologist. It's the only profession that's worth anything. That should be the *only* job in the world. And I'm going to have it.'

My father said, 'It's so wonderful to see that you have ambition, molé.'

My mother said, 'Aiyah, no need to be so . . . so . . . *extreme* lah. Give it a few years. You might like something else.'

'No! Bloody no! Don't you dare tell me what I will do in the future!' Mary shouted, running upstairs, landing a foot on every stair as though she were pushing a brick into an impossible hole.

It was a relief when she began collecting dead grasshoppers in silence.

It went on like that – Mary professing an absolute thought and then reverting to her wordless thought dimension – until, one day, she found a way to multiply her absolutes and take them in, all at once.

'Listen to me!' she said, her voice bleeding with a rusty quality, 'You *have* to see it all! *All*, okay? The morning glories!

The squirrel! The storm! The spirits! God! God! God! He is everywhere! I have found the Lord! The Lord is *not* in the church. The Lord is here in this petal. Look. Take it.'

'That's nice,' my mother replied, taking the purple petal from Mary and dropping it so that it floated like a temporary cradle before landing on the floor, 'Pastor John will be glad to hear you've found the Lord but remember, the Lord is in the church too. Mary, now you must be honest with me. Who is this boy?'

'Oh and the sun talked to me today,' Mary continued as though my mother hadn't spoken. 'It told me that there is only happiness to be found here. Isn't that wonderful? Just wonderful! And last night the moon said to me, "Even in darkness there is light." I am so blessed! Isn't the world just the greatest place in the world?'

Then my father said, 'Mary, why didn't you answer your mother's question? Who is the boy?' His eyes were gaunt and night-like.

But Mary went on. 'The fresh leaves! The soil! The worms! The nests! Orange clouds! Rain! Pineapple! Cobras! Mudswampsfishaloeverawindandstorms!'

For two days, Mary sought the world. She went digging in the garden and collected a colony of earthworms which she left out on the front porch. She took the *tudung saji* from the kitchen and covered her worms with it – an original worm-tent. Then she plucked morning glories, hibiscuses, frangipanis and anthuriums and scattered them in the worm-tent. She jumbled them up, a distinct chop suey. Soon spiders, praying mantises, grasshoppers and dragonflies featured in the fusion. She didn't sleep or eat. She sat by the complex tent, refusing our presence. I wanted to peer into that world she had created but she was its constant guard. All I could see through the gaps of the *tudung saji* were colours. Brash, lonely colours. If she thought she was the only one who could detect wildness, she was wrong.

'You see,' she finally said, 'a voice did come to me. It told me that I have been chosen to rule the planet. What to do? I can't ignore it.' She lifted the *tudung saji*. Joyous flies had joined her world.

'Now, here you see the big mix,' she carried on, 'this big mix is a metaphor for the planet. So I was doing all the work, not knowing that I was actually preparing for my vocation. With my new job, I'll have to have lots of meetings with the public. Daddy, can you arrange this for me?'

My parents secretly drove her to Dr Poh, the only psychiatrist on the island. They took a convoluted route to 'Bright Future Clinic' because in a place like Coal Island, knowledge of mental affliction is seen as more damning than, say, adultery or incest. You'd get more sympathy if you had broken a leg than if you were to admit that your life had been spent trying to ward off an unrecognized illness.

They brought her home that day, saying nothing. My mother made herself a tumbler of Ovaltine and played with her rosary while she stared at the only papaya tree in the garden. My father, having put Mary to bed with a handful of pills, was in the bathroom for hours. Left alone, I sat in my room with a few cans of beer that I had found in the fridge. Each time I looked into my drink and saw the bubbles lift from the base of my glass to gather and dissolve at the surface I thought I understood why bubbles did that. A glittering string, not unlike golden thread, brought me closer towards the bubbles and the holy charms of Carlsberg, where, in that unity, I also understood that Mary and her diseased moods would now sit on the roof of this house and call out to us, asking for relief, for an ear, for our bodies to lie prostrate in devotion.

Mary's illness became the third child and although I was the second child, I was promoted to first rank. Up there, you become a Hercules. The giant is fit to leave home whenever he chooses, is capable of exhuming any kind of resource presented to him and can survive with just his shadow for company. Mary would remain tucked in bed with stacks of pills and her parents' four-dimensional vision that often translated into brutal love. I don't mean brutal in the conventional sense of the word. Basically, they could not give her up. The rice cooker became a perpetual place for porridge, a calming food for the mind. The papayas on the tree were never given a chance to fall from maturity. 'Eat this,' my mother would say, holding a spoonful of mashed papaya near Mary's mouth, 'it will soothe you'. Usually, Mary declined. My father found a new function for his credit card. He fitted a bookshelf in the storeroom and soon, it was filled with books on bipolarity which he repeatedly read and quoted from. Mary's place was with her blanket and the hovering spoon. I don't think she was even allowed to pour a glass of water and drink it.

Slowly, the glimmering string – the one not unlike golden thread – started playing with my new role as the first child, the giant. It knotted itself around me, garnering a lover's warmth when I sat in bed with the bubbles that flattened by the hour, flattening as they did so, my supposed bigness. I was one of those rubber dolls at parades, plump and oily during the show, flying and waving up on the float for a day or two, before the demise begins. The contents, made only of air, cheap, accessible air, seeps away too effortlessly for the way it entered in the first place.

The bubbles and the glimmering string were inevitable friends whenever the weeping from my parents' room became too audible for my liking or when Mary talked on a loop. 'The radio is a beast,' she once said for two hours. My parents were at the market, buying mood-stabilizing foods. 'What radio?' I asked after the first twenty minutes. But I never got to find out which radio she was referring to or why it was a beast. She seemed to be getting worse and I was beginning to detest her, or more specifically, her vague illness. It manifested itself in such diverse ways that I was never able to tell when it was Mary the Person talking. My parents returned from the market and placed a sleeping pill in Mary's water. It was during those quiet moments, when Mary was asleep, that I saw their real faces, marked with lines, even little bubbles, popping up at all corners, anxious to be seen. They often looked beyond me, never directly into my eyes where I wanted them to meet me, because if they had seen what my eyes were made of, they would have discovered only half a son, something no parent wants to encounter.

Two years later Mary was practically bed-bound. They refused to let her exert herself in any way and my mother still fed her porridge in the afternoons and nights and pulped papaya in the evenings. I tried telling them that if they allowed her to do some things for herself, she would feel more alive, more herself. But my mother said, 'This kind of thing ah Kevin, you better leave to the adults.' And so I did.

When I received the letter saying that I had won the scholarship to study History at the University of Manchester, I told my parents that I would be leaving them in a few months. My mother, who was sitting with her rosary in front of the papaya tree, said, 'That's good, boy. You sure you're ready? Daddy and I will miss you very much.' My father nodded and looked away.

'I'm too ready. I can finally go be myself'.

'What do you mean, boy?' my father asked, his face still turned away from mine. He removed a handkerchief and dabbed what turned out to be a few straying tears. I had not realized.

'Nothing. Just that there comes a time when a boy needs to go see the world.'

My father turned to look at me. The tears were gone. 'Yes. You're old enough and you don't need to spend your whole life with parents who have no choice but to give you . . . we . . . I . . . really . . . very . . .'

'We can all be freer now. Just a bit.'

Nobody replied.

I left three months later and arrived in Manchester on a sunless morning, underdressed. The streets were wet and the sky seemed to have a grand stock of water for the next hundred days. I spent my first ten pounds on an extravagant taxi ride from the airport to my flat. The buses were for people who hadn't struggled to get there.

The taxi driver said to me, 'Where ya from, mate? Someplace in Asia I reckon. But I can't quite put my finger on it.'

He was white-haired, unshaven and had a complex map of wrinkles on his face. He made me feel as though when he looked at me he could tell exactly what I was looking for and would use that knowledge to amuse himself when he was waiting for customers.

'Coal Island, I mean, Malaysia.'

'Malaysia! Gorgeous place, gorgeous place. That's next to Vietnam, isn't it?'

'No, Sir. It's above Singapore.'

'Oh yeah, I must have been thinking of some other place. Thailand, it was, yeah, I was thinking about Thailand. Still, I bet it's gorgeous out there. What you doing here, mate? Come to soak up our sun? Heh. Heh.'

'No, Sir. I've come to study.'

'Well, good luck to ya. And try not to get too depressed. Manchester has that habit, you know?'

'No, Sir, I don't.'

The flat was small, cold and overcrowded. There were two bedrooms and three of us which meant that I had to sleep on the futon in the front room where people passed when they needed to use the toilet. My flatmates were English boys who ate out of tins and imagined that we had a special fairy-lady who would one day come to clean the place. 'Don't worry, Kev,' Jon told me when I asked if we should prepare a cleaning rota, 'a lady's gonna come sort us out with this shit. You'll see.' She never did come.

Jon and David were English Literature students at the university but I rarely saw them leaving for class or talking about work and so I concluded that they were either idiots or geniuses. Whatever the reality, they made no effort to explain themselves and I spent less time at home, not really wanting to communicate with them or to witness the rapid build-up of their filth around me. To sleep at night and to forget about the sweat-tipped socks, the half-full pizza boxes, the scattered tins of baked beans, the randomly strewn boxer shorts, I sat in a pub down the road and drank four pints of Stella Artois which always prepared me for my dreams on the futon. Waking up was a different matter. Sobriety jerked me out of bed and I brushed my teeth twice, ignoring the temptation to touch the opened box of Rice Krispies in the kitchen which, if in Malaysia, would have already housed a cockroach or two and a lizard. Breakfast was consumed at my department cafeteria. I ate fried bread, bacon butties, chip butties, crisp sandwiches, anything that could suck the acidity out of my stomach.

At university, I walked on the stony pavements with a rucksack on my back, filled with clothes, a few books, packed sandwiches from the cafeteria, my passport and my toothbrush. I didn't trust that I would automatically return to the flat every night, even though I had nowhere else to go. I did try to make friends with my course mates but our conversations were limited. One of the first people I talked to was a boy named Jim who came from the south of England. 'Hello,' I said, 'I'm Kevin from Malaysia.'

'Kevin? That's not a very Asian name is it?'

'It can be. We have Jims there too.'

'You don't say,' he replied and returned to his book.

I didn't understand the abruptness of their sentences, or the way they called me mate when they had no plans of inviting me out for a pint. And apparently there was something in the way I spoke that made them feel too close to what they really weren't close to. Once I nearly made a friend. Greg, a course mate, said to me while we were waiting for Professor McAdams to arrive, 'You're pretty quiet at tutorials. Do you have a problem understanding?' I didn't think my presence had been analyzed at all. *Somebody* had taken the time to watch me and conclude *something*.

'Oh no. I can understand things. I'm just not comfortable talking when I don't know much.'

'That's not the point though. Everybody's got to have an opinion, mate.'

'What if you don't?'

'Then something's wrong.'

'Wow. I didn't know that.'

'Yeah. Listen, mate, a bunch of us are . . .' His eyes shifted to a group of boys and girls who were standing by the water cooler, arguing, it seemed, about Hitler. He watched them for a while and then said, 'If Germany had won, how would that have impacted Asia?'

I thought about it. I didn't know much about the Second World War. I tried to think of a deceptively informed answer but I couldn't.

'Right then, mate,' Greg continued, 'that's okay.'

'What were the bunch of you going to do?'

'Oh, it's nothing. Really, mate, no worries.'

'You can come to my flat if you like. I'll cook.'

'Seriously, mate, no worries.'

Greg joined the water cooler group and, after that, we communicated through smiles.

I started reading up on European history and recreated various battles in my head, imagining as I did so that I was Nero or Henry VIII or Napoleon. The more I read, the more I remembered the giant I had been.

Every day I would buy a different chocolate bar and write home about it.

'Dear Mummy and Daddy,' I wrote in one email, 'It's a shame that you don't have Aero chocolate in Malaysia. They put bubbles in it. Blimey. One of the benefits I suppose of living in England.'

When I discovered Bounty, I wrote, 'Dear Mummy and Daddy, here's an irony for you. We grow the coconuts but the English have perfected the best coconut chocolate in the world. Wish you could try Bounty. Truly wicked.'

I wanted them to know that I was here, surviving, thriving, involved in every domestic speck of existence in a land of castles, swords, efficient trains and good chocolate. Despite that, I knew that to really flourish, I would have to at least attend a party, tell a successful joke, go to the shops with someone, even – if I could flourish that much – wake up next to a white body. But Jon and David, the only real English people who spoke to me (if only to find out whether the milk had gone sour or if I had a spare razor), were too self-contained to welcome me into their world of processed food and exhibitionist masturbation. Besides, we had known each other for almost a year and to throw my friendliness at them after so long would be like producing a delayed reaction to a piece of tragic news.

I had lost my chance at university as well. I was the shy Asian boy who was able to impersonate rulers of the past in a creepy way and I could not undo that impression. The local pub I frequented, The Horse and the Kettle, was often empty and even when there were people, they were men over the age of sixty. I ran out of chocolate bars to test and I moved on to Cornish pasties. But this strategy of thriving or flourishing or whatever it was that I was hoping to achieve through my supermarket experiments was depressing me.

Then I gave up the tasting sessions and Gemma walked into The Horse and Kettle on a late Thursday night. She was small for an Englishwoman. She had the build of a Chinese girl but she was pure white, like a jasmine flower or fresh milk (not the powdered kind). Her eyes were hard green but they produced a soft effect, making them out to be something like floor pillows. She sat next to me at the bar and ordered a glass of red wine, all the while, I imagined, aware of my presence. I could see her fingers tapping on the counter top and at the base of her glass while her eyes pretended to stay focused on the beer taps in front of her. But she was watching me with eyeballs that could sink to the lowest region of the eye and spy from there.

I remember saying before I could stop myself, 'Good evening, Madam. It's a pleasant night.'

The tapping stopped. Without looking at me, she replied to the soiled pub air, 'Is it?' She twisted a few tendrils of her ginger hair and drank her half-full glass of wine in one apparent gulp.

'Another?' I asked.

'Sure, why not? I did come here to get plastered, after all.'

When the next glass arrived she finished it within a few minutes and I felt compelled to buy her another and another until her lips became blackened with the red of the wine and her mouth gave off an odour of rancid fruit.

'What's . . . who're you?' she demanded while she rested her head on my shoulder.

'Kevin. Madam, do you live close by?'

'Some . . . where. Over there, you know. Close? I dunno. I'm Gemma. Maybe. I'll be okay.'

I took her back to my flat and put her to bed on the futon. I slept on the floor dressed in four jumpers, long johns and two pairs of trousers but I still shivered and so I decided to stay up. I sat in the dark, thinking about Gemma, the only woman to have felt the rough fabric of my futon and who breathed like a child who'd had a long day of play. She was older – I guessed maybe fifteen years? – but she was more beautiful than any girl my age I'd known and not known. I was still thinking about her when she woke up and asked me if we had slept together.

'Of course not, Madam.'

'Oh, would you please stop with the Madam? I know Asians are into the whole respect thing but, frankly, it makes me feel old.'

'Alright, Gemma. What would you like for breakfast? We have baked beans and tea. Out of bread, I'm afraid.'

'Boys. They just can't bear to live decently, can they? How about I take you out for breakfast as a thank you for not letting me sleep on a park bench like a regular tramp? And get me a glass of water, will you? My head's killing me.'

Gemma and I ended up spending the entire day together at a cafe, talking.

'So, Malaysia, huh?' she said, her floor pillow eyes fixed on the sky. I couldn't see what was so grabbing there. It wasn't blue. It had no clouds. She must have been associating it with something else, something finer, more delicious.

'Yes. Have you ever been?'

'No. But someday . . . I have this vision of me with a backpack, trailing the hot streets of Thailand, Malaysia, India, buying sweets at stalls, drinking tea with men and women who don't understand what I'm saying but that would be the least of their concerns, you know?'

'You can do that in Malaysia, on Coal Island. I'll show you.' Her thighs were pink and shiny. She could endure the cold even when they were that bare. I let my hands fall on them, taking in her warmth.

'Really? You would? You're such a sweet boy.'

'Of course I would. I can take you to the night markets and the villages and you can drink all the tea you like. We have pulled tea. They stretch out the tea. Up and down it goes.'

'How marvellous. You're really very handsome, you know. Like a Hindu god.'

'I'm half Chinese.'

'Even better.'

When the cafe closed, we returned to the Horse and Kettle and drank as we had done the night before but Gemma insisted on going home despite her condition.

'What if you pass out?' I said, stroking her arm. She squeezed my upper thigh and then, in a dash, landed her hand on my crotch.

'Well, my love, I simply can't afford to faint along the way. My husband will be wondering what's happened to me.'

I couldn't imagine Gemma being married to anybody. If she had to be someone's wife, she'd be mine. Perhaps they were on their way to an amicable divorce.

'You weren't home last night. He didn't call or care. Why'd he bother tonight?'

'Oh, John'll care, of course he will. Last night he was in Paris for a conference. Tonight he's expecting me by his side.'

'But . . . you mean, you're happy with this man?'

'He's my childhood sweetheart, so yes. Been together twenty-five years.'

'So you do this often then? Flirt with other men and then return to dependable John?'

'Never done it in my life. Feeling the guilt now of course. I'm not sure what this is but my poor John. He'd . . . he'd . . . oh I don't know what he'd do if he knew what I was doing. But I dunno, there's something about you. It's like we've been together in a past life. I could've been Asian.'

'You liked kissing me?'

'Yes. Now I must go. I really must.'

'Can we meet again? Please, Gemma. You're my . . . I've never felt like this, like a man . . . who's . . . who's looked at by a woman.'

'Oh dear god. I don't know what I'm doing. John'll . . . John'll . . . I don't know *what* John'll. I want to. I do, I do want to see you again.'

'Then meet me here tomorrow night.'

Her face looked like a flower that moves rapidly through the stages of transition from a mere bud to a fully realized thing of its own. I knew she wasn't lying and yet the situation was impossible.

'Yes. Okay. But why don't we just meet at your place? I'll bring the wine.'

After that, whenever John was out of the house Gemma came to the flat. Usually, we sat on my futon and talked. She was a housewife who loved baking bread but hated other domestic activities. John didn't mind. He laughed off her homemaking inadequacies and even when they found out that she had a hostile womb he explained that it wasn't her womb that he had married. Every time she mentioned him I felt something cold and sharp spin around in my body but there was nothing I could do to stop her from admiring her own husband. When she wasn't talking about John, she mentioned her various ambitions: to travel and eat breads from around the world, to live in a warm climate, to write her own cookbook, to be free.

It's strange how I only discovered who John was two months into our affair. She talked about him at great length but I never asked her any questions about him until one day I said, 'So what is it that John does? You know, for a living.'

'Oh, he's a professor in History at Manchester Uni.'

It was my fault, I suppose. We could have found out sooner if I hadn't banned the subject of my studies from our conversations. 'Please tell me it's not John McAdams.'

'That's the one.'

He was the gentlest, cleverest man I had ever met. In fact, his were the only classes I loyally attended and he had been the one to assert that I had the intelligence to write a concise History of the World. I wasn't sure what he meant by that but I accepted the compliment and went away delighted.

'So poor John is your professor,' Gemma said, 'and here I am playing nookie with one of his boys. How awful. But I can't help it. I love you, Kevin. And I love John.'

'You know you can't have both. This whole thing isn't healthy.'

'Of course I know that. Look, now it's become worse . . . worse than when I was just keeping a secret from John. It's a larger secret. An infinite secret.'

'And what now?'

'I'm going home and running myself a bath. That's where I do all my thinking.'

I let her go, feeling desperate, contained, stunned. I wanted to write to my parents to tell them that my life had become a life. Instead I wrote to Kumar.

> Hey Kumar,
>
> You're not going to believe this. I don't know how it happened. The whole thing is crazy but . . . here it is: I'm

> involved with a married woman! I met her at my local pub and she's twenty years my senior. She's gorgeous. Pale skin, green eyes, red hair. Damn exotic. Now, you'll never guess who her husband is. Wait for it . . . my History Professor! This all seems like it belongs to a movie or a novel but believe it or not, it's my life. What should I do?

After two days, Kumar's email arrived.

> Kevin,
> I know you're excited about this soap opera but we're talking about actual lives here. Don't do it. You're ruining more than you think.

But one week later Gemma announced that she was divorcing John. 'We'll get a place together,' she said, 'I've some money and . . . if things get bad I can always go on the dole and get housing benefit. This is a new life for me, for us, two people from different countries, two different age groups, two different . . . different *everything*. This could be good, Kev, I just have a hunch about it. East and West. Me and You. It's beautiful, isn't it?'

We moved into a one-bedroom flat and when Professor McAdams found out who his wife had left him for he stopped speaking to me. Surprisingly, my grades remained the same. Life with Gemma was a life I had never lived before. The flat became a place for everything that the outside world was too weak to give. There were the occasional weeping sessions for John and I pretended that those sobs and sniffles didn't exist because every time they emerged, I became nothing at all. But, on the whole, we were happy.

In my final year at uni, I said to Gemma, 'Not long left till my visa expires. How's this going to work?'

'You'll get a job.'

'And if I don't?'

'I don't know then.'

'Marry me.'

'I can't. I'm still legally married to John.'

'Why is that taking so long?'

'These things take time.'

'When it goes through, will you marry me?'

'Oh please don't make this hard. I don't think it's advisable to jump from one marriage to the next.'

'You're still in love with him aren't you?'

'I'll always love him. Twenty-five years. It's not easy to just drop everything and move on. I didn't leave him because I stopped loving him. I left because I fell in love with someone else.'

'What am I to you?'

'You're my lover.'

'Then marry me.'

'It's not that simple.'

'It can be. Please, Gemma. What if I can't stay? I'll be in Malaysia and you'll be here. How can I be in your life if I'm miles away?'

'I'm too old for you.'

'You've never been too old for me. Why start now?'

'Reality's reality. John's mature and secure, I mean, financially. Look at us. We're struggling.'

'But that's love.'

'I had love with John too and we didn't suffer.'

'Then go back to him. Why do you have to waste our lives if you're planning to be stuck on him until you die?'

'You need to grow up. When you've spent twenty-five years with someone, then you'll know.'

'I plan to do that with you.'

'But I've already done that. Can't you see? I've already experienced what you're waiting to experience. Maybe this won't work.'

'But I love you.'

'And I love you. You were born too late, my love. It's sad. It'll always be sad.'

'What are you saying?'

'I've been thinking. John says he forgives me and things are so uncertain with you and me. You might not even be in this country for much longer and I need a life, a real one, Kev Kevs. We've been good together but . . .'

'I get it. You're going back to your husband. You're leaving me. You don't care. You don't give a damn what happens to me. I could rot on Coal Island for all you care.'

'It sounds like a lovely place. Why do you hate it so much?'

'People pretend to care and families are corrupt there. I'll go back to parents who can only think about their mad daughter. They've rarely mentioned her in the three years I've been here and I've never asked. I can only imagine. She's gone madder. The last thing my parents said about her was that she's been wanting to murder the iguanas in the drain. How can I go back to that? Tell me.'

'Maybe she has good reason to murder iguanas. Has anybody ever asked her why? Anyway, you'll start your own life apart from your family. You're a big boy now. You'll find a girl your own age and get married like John and I did.'

'Please, Gemma.'

'Kev Kevs, don't make this hard. I've made up my mind. I'm going back to my husband.'

When I returned to Malaysia months later my parents seemed grateful to have me back but I was not able to feign interest in them or in my sister. I didn't feel ready for a job. I didn't think working with a maimed heart would get me very far. So I stayed in my room and dreamt about England while the monochrome wheel began turning again and the glimmering string reappeared.

One day when my parents were out visiting a relative I went to see Mary. My task was to feed her lunch and then tuck her in but she was talking. Mary's talking was not simple talking. It was talking upon talking.

'One iguana. Two iguanas. Sitting in the drain. Causing me this pain. Kevin, please get them, please, please, please. One iguana. Two iguanas. Sitting in the drain. Causing me this pain.'

'What have the iguanas ever done to you?' I thought about what Gemma had said. Maybe all someone needed to do was to ask her why.

'They eat our shit in the drain. I don't like that they know what I taste like. They lick our shit and they eat our shit and they shit our shit. And I don't like that they know what I taste like.'

'That's true, I suppose. But what are you going to do about it?'

'Listen here. They are dirty. They have no respect. Our shit is not meant to be their food. We have to catch them.' Her voice had turned hard. Suddenly, she looked fierce, secure, determined through understanding.

'I can't just catch them. I don't know how.'

'Iguanas can be fast when they sense danger so you must look innocent. Take a rope, make it into a lasso and throw it over them when they cannot see you.'

She had thought the whole thing out. She said she had been planning it for the last year. I could not, even if I tried to, see her madness. What I saw was a girl who was upset that a part of her was exposed to underground creatures. It was as if she believed that her soul lingered in her shit and because the iguanas were eating her shit, they were also getting at her soul. All she wanted to do was to recover herself.

'You have to do it, Kevin, for both of us.'

'Why both of us?'

'You know why.'

That afternoon I performed my sister's instructions. She even followed me to the garden, something my parents never allowed her to do, and we waited for the iguanas together. We sat for hours while the reptiles loitered invisibly beneath us.

'Why aren't you happy?' she asked.

'I hate this place. I hate Coal Island. I want to be back in Manchester.'

'What are you running away from?'

I was surprised at her question.

'The island lah . . . and all of its . . . *stuff*.'

'What's so great about Manchester?'

'I was free and I had a person who actually saw me like she saw me and liked what she saw.'

'I like what I see when I look at you.'

We heard the movements of the iguanas. They were rising.

'What do you see?'

'A boy who can't see himself. A perfectly formed stem that cannot take the wind and so must be protected.'

'How can you see like that?'

'I just can.'

The iguanas were making their way to the centre of the drain, a few inches away from where we sat.

'Slowly now,' she whispered, 'take the lasso and gently throw it over. You take the left one. I'll take the right.'

The creatures didn't put up a fight. We tightened the lassos and tied the iguanas to the porch pillar.

'What do you want to do with them?' I asked.

'Sell them to Mummy's side of the family. The Chinese will eat anything,' she said.

I laughed. 'Better still. We cook a curry out of them, send it to Daddy's side of the family and tell them it's chicken. The Indians are too stupid to know.'

She laughed. We decided to release them back into the drain so that we could sit in the garden with our lassos the next day and repeat the catch. It would be our new game, as though we were children again, hunters in the wild.

10

Parrot Love

HIS NAME WAS Ribut which in Malay means 'storm'. He grew up in an orphanage and there was no way of knowing why his parents named him that. He wore pantaloons and fitted T-shirts and when he smiled a deep dimple appeared on his left cheek. We were in love for 271 days.

I teach yoga at the Leisure Centre every evening and this is where we met. Ribut showed up with a mat and a parrot on his shoulder. I told him, 'Sir, the bird has to wait in the corner.'

The parrot lifted one wing, as though it were about to slap itself, and yowled. I didn't think birds were capable of such earth-shattering anger.

'Enough, Fifi,' he said, 'let's just go.'

As he was leaving, I saw the way his ponytail trailed down his back like a thick worm clinging on to a wall, and a strange thought came to me. 'I don't know why,' I said to myself, 'but I have a feeling this man might take Rocky away for good.' It was wrong, sure, seeing that he hardly had a wrinkle on his face – not even lines to indicate that some laughter had been produced to make life more manageable – but we do not control such things. The heart is an automaton sometimes. It just moves.

'Actually, come to think of it,' I shouted just before he had completed his journey down the stairs, 'I'm sure the parrot will be fine if we don't do the rolling exercises.'

I wasn't certain, but I thought I heard Fifi say, 'Bitch'.

Ribut returned daily. The mirrored yoga room allowed me to observe him without coming across as intense. His narrow frame, filled in with minimal flesh, was complimented by his height. He looked elongated, as if someone had hooked him to a coconut tree, and his back bent just like a crow's beak. He reminded me of someone, or some *type* of condition. It was a very old condition, I decided. Yes, he was a man who could watch the folds of his cave for hours.

If Rocky was thick-armed, curly-haired and chesty, then Ribut embodied the antonyms of those descriptions. Is it possible to love two opposites? Fat-short-dark-mouthy. Thin-tall-fair-nearly mute. Or perhaps I myself had evolved. After all, I was only twenty-five when Rocky asked for a divorce.

Just two years before, he had taken me to a deserted lake and whisked a creased sunflower out of his pocket. Then he sang, in the tune of 'Chariots of Fire', 'Lily, oh, Lily, Lils, my dear Lils, marry me yar.' He was down on both knees and his face had become the whole ocean.

'No, no, Rocks, I haven't even got a job,' I said.

'Job? Why do you need a job? I can do everything for you yar,' he said.

Still, I replied, 'We're too young lah.'

But every month after that he asked again. And again. And again. It was getting embarrassing. I said, 'Okay. Fine. I mean, I *do* love you.' So how was it that seven months later he woke me up and said, 'Lily, I want a divorce?' Just like that. I had spent those seven months in our home for *him*. I scrubbed and ironed his underwear.

'Why all of a sudden?' I asked.

He replied curtly, as though I were a beggar asking for coins, 'You're smothering me.'

Smothering? Smothering? What did that even *mean*? Then he left and my body turned cold until I heard that he was walking around town with a ponytailed lawyer. I simply couldn't stay in Ipoh. So I closed my eyes, pointed my index finger on a map of Malaysia, opened my eyes and found Coal Island. I didn't tell Rocky I was leaving and I didn't hear from him.

But Rocky did come with me to the island. I never kissed a man because of him. He was everywhere I went. The moment I thought I liked a man, I'd see Rocky. Ribut seemed to dismiss Rocky's ghost. What talent he had.

'Ribut,' I said, a few weeks after he started attending my yoga classes, 'you're getting so good at yoga lah. Soon you can start giving your own classes!'

That was when he said, 'I'd rather not take away income from the woman I love.'

A week later, Ribut moved into my house. He had been

living with four friends in a small apartment near town and I wanted to make sure that he, at the age of twenty-five, did not have to relive his orphanage days.

We loaded my truck with his things (a rubbish bag of clothes and a suitcase of art materials) and within minutes my extra cupboard was no longer vacant.

'Is that all? No kitchenware?' I asked.

'My whole big existence can be filled in one black rubbish bag,' he replied, 'isn't that enough?' Ribut never seemed to care about what hung on him or the accessories that went with life. He could walk around with a cloth around his waist. He didn't do that, of course, but he did prefer T-shirts over shirts, no underwear over underwear.

On weekday evenings we had our dinner beneath a tree at a nearby park. 'For dinner we will have sandwiches. No margarine. Just brown bread and cucumber,' he told me.

'Bread and cucumber for dinner every night, Ribs?' I asked.

'Yes, why, you have a problem with that?'

'Oh, no, no, no, no, no.'

Ribut's style was good for me, I thought. Now, I would *really* appreciate nice-smelling soap, even a good old-fashioned penholder. It was probably time that I gave up butter, meat, cream and cocoa.

At lunch, Ribut chewed on his boiled potatoes as though the pleasure they were giving him could not be named. Then he would pick a broccoli floret and suck at it, fishing out its nectar. The way he grazed a carrot cube with his teeth was beautiful to watch. I stopped storing salt in the house.

On Saturdays, Ribut and I would have a picnic at the

beach. 'Now, for our picnics,' he said, 'we will take a large Tupperware of cut celery, green bell peppers, radish, onions and pineapple. Toss them all up. Sprinkle a bit of cumin. Bring along a bottle of Spritzer mineral water. 1,500 ml.'

Even if I had wanted to embellish the menu a bit, I would never shame myself in front of him. I thought about the benefits of champagne, chicken cold cuts and black olives but it was no use. No. A sip of water *could* taste like Asti if you closed your eyes hard enough and remembered when you were young, drinking Asti alone in your room, just because the night had come. In any case, it was not for the food and drinks that we had our weekly picnics.

We parked ourselves at the very end of the stretch of sand near a large wrinkled rock. 'This here, do you see it?' he said on our first picnic, pointing at the obvious rock, 'this is not just a rock. It is "The Sensitive Curtain of Love". You'll soon see why.' He looked into my eyes like a baby deer that discovers the wonders of shoots for the first time. A mass of energy – love, I'm pretty sure it was – left his body and entered mine. It was one of those moments when you are unbelievably, sincerely, shocked by the simple fact of being human. You are able to perform ordinary miracles from your heart and eyes and fingers.

We placed an old bed sheet behind 'The Sensitive Curtain of Love' and Ribut touched my hips, then my thighs, my belly. He pushed me to the ground and I curled into him. Every Saturday, I curled into him. Fifi would stand by the salad container, guarding, watching. It wasn't that I had anything against the parrot but when she said, 'Go, Go,

Goal!' my shoulders seemed to push out of my skin. I tried talking to Ribut about leaving Fifi at home on Saturdays but the second time I mentioned it he said, 'Eh, don't undermine the parrot. Where I go, she goes.' I wondered whether it was conducive for our relationship to have Fifi judge it. Once she blurted out, 'One is young, one is old, one has sung, the other on hold. How can love like this, ah?' From the question I realized that she had picked it up from some fishwife. The parrot's sense of hearing and of repeating was precocious. But since it was clear that the only way to keep Ribut was to accept the parrot, I blocked out her words.

I kept them in the house as much as I could so that she would not have the opportunity to pick up on more conversations. Places like the market, the Leisure Centre and the Coal Island Recreational Club were particularly damaging.

'I'll do the shopping, Ribs, you just rest,' I said, 'Oh, and don't worry about going to the Leisure Centre. We'll just do yoga at home. Together.'

'Good job, Lily. I like how you're freeing up my hours. Now I can draw in peace. Really, Lily, good job.'

My inner body bubbled. I could hear it, like a peaking cauldron, rising, rising towards some *kind* of destination. It was an intolerably beautiful place, I decided. Days passed and the place acquired 1,000-watt lights, floral drapery, Chinese lanterns with golden stars. Ribut had a way of bringing me towards his chest and cupping my head in his hands so that I could feel the warmth *inside* the earth. He liked playing with only one strand of my hair, and before he tugged it out, my skin heaved like water does after a fat person has left the bathtub.

As our relationship became more intense and less peopled, the parrot grew quiet. She still shouted, 'Go, Go, Goal!' at the beach but I was already used to that despite the pain in my shoulders.

Then things changed. When Ribut and I celebrated our 264th-day anniversary with a baked chicken (he even allowed me to dab some olive oil on its skin) and Cascade cordial, the parrot sat silently on Ribut's shoulder, its eyes half shut, its beak slightly tilted downwards. It looked a little depressed to me but I wasn't going to bring up the subject of its well-being on our special day.

'Ribs,' I said, 'how lucky we are, isn't it? To have all this? Not many people get to find a person they love so much.'

He raised his glass of cordial up in the air, smiled and put it back on the table.

'You think we have a future?' I continued, feeling an uncommon happiness as I watched the parrot nod off, 'I know what people are saying about . . . about, aiyah you know lah what they are saying, those nasty . . . ah, why should we bother about them anyway, right?'

He smiled and raised his glass again, this time higher up in the air than before. 'Who is saying what?' he said.

'You know my yoga class is much smaller now than it was last year,' I replied, 'but who cares? The point is that we have found each other. So . . . you think we have a future?'

Ribut stroked Fifi with a finger but the parrot didn't move. 'Ya, of course. But, Lily, you must make sure you keep your job. How else would we survive? I'm trying but no one wants to buy my drawings. If we're going to get married, this family will have to depend on you.'

The moment he said the word 'married' my whole body went smooth like a roll of silk material that had been laid and evened out on a table by a pair of dedicated hands. I understood his struggle as an artist and I didn't mind that he was producing art that no one was interested in. The greatest artists had to wait for centuries before they clung onto fame and never let go. I didn't know much about art but I was sure Ribut was talented. He had to be.

'Oh, Ribs,' I said, 'Anything, I'll do anything to have you in my life. I promise to support this family. I'll reduce the rates of my yoga class. I'm sure people won't care about my personal life if they can do yoga cheaply. Does this mean we're getting married?'

Ribut stood up and called me to him. I went. He kissed me on the forehead and whispered into my ear, 'Ya, sure.'

I noticed that the parrot still wasn't moving, and although I wanted to ignore it and celebrate Ribut's (sort of) marriage proposal to me, I worried that if anything happened to Fifi, Ribut would never recover and the whole wedding would be called off. So I said, 'Ribs, I'm sure it's nothing but why is Fifi so still?'

He laughed and replied, 'Every once in a while she goes into some kind of hibernation. Parrots are not supposed to do this but my Fifi, well, she's special. When she wakes up she's usually more alert than before. More clever. It takes a few days. You'll see.'

The news was wonderful. The parrot could not ruin my day. It's true that she had become a lot quieter since I started doing all the shopping and we stopped meeting too many people but she was still capable of repeating words, phrases and conversations from the distant past. A short while before her hibernation, she had said, 'Ribs, even garlic? What's wrong with garlic? Garlic? It's the enemy. Don't you notice how you smell when you eat it? Have you gone close to a garlic fart? Garlic makes the blood hot. Really? Yes. So no more garlic.'

I thought it would be best if we had the wedding during this peculiar period of hibernation. I didn't particularly like the idea of Fifi interrupting the ceremony with her wise words. But Ribut insisted on waiting for the Terror of Feathers (I had started calling her that in my head without Ribut's knowledge) to awaken because he wanted her to present him with the ring. Then I had to ask him something I had forgotten to ask during our days together. 'Are you a Muslim?' I said.

Ribut threw his head back and laughed like a scheming salesman. 'What do you think?'

'I mean . . . your name . . . well, it's *in* Malay but it's not exactly *Muslim*. And your face . . . your face is *so* Malay. But I just want to say lah that I don't care even if you are Muslim. I'll convert. I'll do it. I'll do anything for you.'

'It's funny how you never bothered to ask. How can you be so sure that someone called Ribut can't be a Punjabi or a Chinese?'

'It's . . . it's not that. I mean, look at you.'

'Me? My father was Eurasian, my mother Chinese. I don't know how I was named.'

'Well, well. Look at how blind people can be sometimes. That's what love does. It gives you half-hearted eyes. Oh, Ribut! I'm so happy. I mean, I would've done it, I promise. But now it's easier.'

That day I went into town to look for a bridal gown. I wanted to be discreet because I wasn't prepared to hear the usual talk about my relationship with Ribut. I never really stopped to listen of course but I would catch shreds of information: Cradle Snatcher, Mrs Robinson, Sugar Mama. But at the bridal shop I bumped into Josie D'Cruz and her heavily pregnant daughter Daisy.

'Lily!' Josie said, her eyeballs crooked and disconcerting. She must have started drinking again, I thought. Her husband's second heart attack had really affected her.

'Josie. Daisy. Nice to see you. What brings you here?'

'Our Daisy's baby is going to have a proper father, that's what.'

'Wonderful. Congratulations, Daisy. Who's the groom? Someone special, I'm sure.'

'Thank you, Auntie Lily,' Daisy said, rotating two fingers on her belly, 'Amitabh Kannan. We're getting married in a few months. And you?'

'Don't be silly, Daisy,' Josie jumped in, 'we all know who Auntie Lily is marrying. It's that boy with the parrot. Well Lily, all I can say is good luck to you. And . . . and . . . shame on you!'

They hurried out of the shop and I stood in front of the

white dresses wondering if Josie D'Cruz was the right person to accuse me of shamelessness. I stayed a while because the saleslady was friendly enough to me and she smiled a lot. I left the shop with a nice white dress in my hands.

When I arrived home Ribut was taking a nap and as I sat down at the kitchen table to have a glass of water I saw an envelope addressed to me lying on the chair along with bills that Ribut had failed to tell me about. I recognized the thick handwriting, like a child's, a deeply eager child's. 'Rocky, Rocky,' I whispered as I opened the envelope. My body was getting cold again as it had done years ago when I gave up being Mrs Rocky Thilagarajah. The letter read:

> Dear Lily,
> It has taken me years to find you. Who would have thought that you would have chosen a quiet life on a dull little island? People make their own choices, I suppose. I'm going to make this brief. I need to see you. Please be open to my visit. I really need to see you. I'll be there on 1st July.
> Take care, Rocky.

I didn't tell Ribut about Rocky's visit. I'm not sure why. Perhaps it was because I had never actually told Ribut that I had been married before. I didn't want him to think of me as a *divorcee*. Plus, that was old news. It happened when I was around Ribut's age and my life had become something entirely new.

Why was Rocky visiting me *now*? Had he sensed, through some love-radar, that I was getting married again? And he wanted me back. Oh, Rocky wanted me back! He had never stopped loving me just as I had always kept him somewhere inside myself for reference, for hope, for a little taste of my past. If Rocky asked me to move back to the mainland with him I would give up everything on Coal Island. But Ribut, Ribut, my poor, young, orphaned, parrot-loving Ribut. Maybe life with him would even be difficult, in a way that was different to how it was with Rocky. Ribut would love me and then retreat into a space that only Fifi had access to – a space of contradictions, both wild and silent, mysterious and yet completely there. Rocky would not show his love but I would feel it in a look, in the way his hand fell comfortably on my back when he was asleep in bed and I watched him.

I sent Ribut on a long list of errands on 1st July. The parrot was comatose so it was acceptable for him to be out among people. I waited at home, nervous, delighted, on the brink of feeling everything that I was capable of. And then the car arrived. Rocky stepped out, older, more handsome, his hands in his pockets, a little shy, a little anxious as he should have been.

'You're looking well-toned yar, Lils,' he said as he slapped me on the back.

'I should be. I teach yoga. And you . . . you don't look your age. Do you dye your hair or something?'

He did look at least ten years younger than he was. There was something about him – a glimmer, a restless electricity – that made him seem superior to everybody else. I loved him. It was difficult not to.

'Well, come in,' I said, thinking about the kiss we would

soon have, 'how about a drink? I have Cascade cordial and water.'

'No, thanks. I don't plan on staying long.' He looked around the room uncomfortably. 'Lils, you never signed the divorce papers yar. I've been trying to find you for the past year. I didn't actually care before. But now I'm getting married again and I need you to sign them yar.'

I looked at him, thinking about the time I had spent taking care of him only to be punched in the face with the word 'smothering'. He was doing it again. He was taking away what I wanted to give. But I still had Ribut. Rocky, Rocky, ah, he had never been a rock. He would just never want me.

'Congratulations,' I said, 'it's a damn good thing you came. I'd be committing bigamy if you didn't! Because you see, Rocky, I too am getting married. To a man twenty years younger. Twenty. Imagine. Still got my charm, I guess.'

'Wowee,' his eyes shone with that electricity, 'that's fantastic news yar! And here's the irony. My girl, well, she's twenty years younger too! Both families are overjoyed. My parents are so, so happy to have a fresh, young daughter-in-law and hers are glad to have a stable son-in-law. Well, Lils, looks like we've finally done well for ourselves yar.'

There certainly was irony in this whole thing. What would Josie D'Cruz have said about Rocky's marriage? Nothing. 'How lovely,' perhaps.

'That's right, Rocky, good for us. I can't believe it slipped my mind that I never signed. Now where are those papers?'

Ribut returned a couple of hours after Rocky had left. 'Done it all,' he said, 'now for some rest.'

'Ribs, we should get registered soon.'

'Sure, sure. We'll talk about that some other time. Have your yoga classes recovered?'

'Ya, my plan worked. I guess people here are cheap after all.'

'Good. So happy to hear.'

That's when it happened. The parrot opened her eyes and Ribut was right. She was more alive than before. She talked and talked and talked.

'Ribut,' she said, 'we are so lucky to have each other. Love is all we need. Oh, Lily, yes of course. But Lily, we should drink at least twelve glasses of water a day. Please don't put oil in the salad when I'm not looking. Ribut, a little oil is good. No oil. No oil. I wonder, Fifi, if she brings home all the money she gets at the Centre. She can be stingy sometimes. I can't say I love her. Have you seen those wrinkles? Hee Hee Hee. Ah, Fifi, at least we'll be fed now, eh? And I can draw, my love, I can draw.'

I never saw Ribut again after that day. I didn't realize how much wildness I had in me. To dismiss two loves in a day is something only people with laminated hearts can do. And yet, I had done it.

I haven't stopped loving Rocky and Ribut. I think about them often when I'm doing the laundry or ironing clothes. Every day I sit myself down on my bed and say to my wedding dress, 'Whatever the kind of love, it's the same thing. It can die at any time. My husband will come when I expect the world of him and when my hands can only be used to take the last cent from his pocket.'

11

The Bat Whisperer

I OWN THE best stocked supermarket on Coal Island. It belonged to my father who handed it down to me when he died. He was an angry man because he had no sons and was stuck with a single daughter. But, in his own way, I think he loved me. He used to scold my mother often. 'Ramona, you good for nothing woman! Only a woman like you can't bear boys!' he'd say and she'd stay silent while looking at her toes. No wonder she died years before he did. Who wants to be reminded that they're worthless by their own husband? It was my mother who inspired me to remain a spinster. What if I had inherited her cold womb? Boys never liked me, anyway. They used to sing, 'Fatty, Fatty, Fatihah, looking for food, pig smells good.' At the age of ten I weighed fifty kilograms. Now, I'm sixty years old and touching ninety. My fat keeps me warm and calm. What I look like doesn't matter anymore since I'm a supermarket matriarch and am entering old age. Not once have I regretted taking on the shop. It's the most revealing place on the island.

A large woman with soft, moist, safe eyes behind a supermarket counter is the best target for sad, lonely or guilty people out to buy a tin of tuna and a bottle of Coke. At times, from my corner in the shop, I can detect those who have come in for practical purposes and those who place a packet of Maggi Mee on the counter and want to tell me about how they had poisoned the neighbour's cat or fought with their husband. I just have to say, 'How are you?' and they begin. I listen but give no advice. I don't want that kind of responsibility. But somehow, that's enough for them. My presence is all they need. I learnt my lesson when Roseleana Khamis came in one day, supposedly for a box of Fab washing powder. After paying, she lingered by the counter for a while before saying, 'Fatihah, I don't know what to do lah. I can't stand working at the club anymore. The people there . . . Ya Allah! I think I should leave. What you think?' I had heard many things about the Coal Island Club and I pitied her so I said, 'Then leave lah. Nobody stopping you what.' She quit her job and I hear the family can't even afford to pay the electricity bill because she decided to go back to school. They live by candlelight. If I had said, 'Keep the job. Think of your family,' at least little Rahman wouldn't be wearing pyjamas to social functions.

But it's not always easy to say nothing. It really depends on what story's being told. For instance, when Mrs Teng comes in I know that what she has to say is not about her and so it's fine for me to comment. She only talks about others and I'm not sure whether she speaks the truth. I will admit, though, that she's a talented gossip and I'm always a bit excited when she drops by. Sometimes, of course, what she says can be upsetting but even more than that is *how* she does it. When she told me about Chan Hui Yong's bastard pregnancy with a dirty smile on her face, I wondered how someone could be so happy about a half-orphaned girl's bad luck. But Mrs Teng has been a source of some of the most intriguing pieces of news. Not long ago she claimed that Tan Pong Pong had announced three remarkable things. Firstly, that he was gay. Secondly, that he was Hindu. Thirdly, that he was a bat whisperer. 'A what?' I asked Mrs Teng who was laughing as though she were choking. 'This man,' she said, 'always so weird one. That one we know lah. But who know how weird lah, Fatihah? He been sitting in that temple for months with poor old Devaki Menon. People say they having sex relation in front of the god. I think so he got fed up. Then he tell Meenachi Muthu he like men and is one Hindu so she should stop tell lies about him and Devaki Menon and stop ask him why he go to temple. Then suddenly he say that if anyone got bat problem to call him. He say that he find a way to talk to bats so if people got bat in their roof or whatever, he can go ask them to leave. This kind of talent people call whispering. My daughter say, like the movie 'The Horse Whisperer'. At first I thought, people will do anything for a few extra ringgit. But Mrs Teng said that Pong Pong wasn't asking for money in return for his work. I found myself wishing for bats inside my roof.

The shop was quiet for a few days. Only one or two minor

incidents happened like Vani Muthu referring to Mrs Mano as a bitch but refusing to say why and *Pak Cik* Khamis slipping a tin of corn into a torn plastic bag. When the tin fell out, I pretended not to notice but unfortunately, just at that moment, Mrs Teng walked in and reported *Pak Cik* Khamis to me. I simply said, 'I told *Pak Cik* to take it lah.' I still felt guilty for his daughter's return to school at the age of forty. Mrs Teng had not much more news to broadcast or any updates on the bat whisperer. Whenever the island has no gossip to offer, you have to be careful if you happen to see Mrs Teng. The woman has a way of asking questions to get the answers she needs so that her gossip tank will be refilled. In the days before the bat whisperer was heard of again, she came into my shop every morning. She would smile sweetly, scan the row of biscuits and chocolates, move her hand across the wrappers, pick up a packet as though she really needed more Julie's sandwich cream wafers and stand in front of my counter, still smiling, waiting to spill her curiosity all over me.

'So Fatihah,' she said recently, 'not bored ah? Everyday also sit here and wait for customer. You should make hobby. Collect stamp or something lah. Actually, if you get one pet is better. Now I think ah, you also alone at home. Wah, how you do it?'

I had never doubted that living and working alone was my fate. I didn't want a pet cat to change that. Besides, I had seen how lonely people became so attached to their kept animals that they would slowly forget to identify human beings. 'No lah, Mrs Teng,' I replied, 'I'm quite happy where I am. But thanks for asking.' The smile grew an inch shorter.

'I see,' she quickly said, 'how come you never marry, ah?' It didn't take much for Mrs Teng to rip the layers of social politeness that we take pains to maintain. For her, they were just pieces of unimportant decoration.

I knew the game she was playing and so I answered, carefully, 'I never wanted to get married. That's three ringgit and twenty cents for the cream wafers.'

By that point, the smile had vanished altogether and she handed the money over with a cold hand. I thought I wouldn't see her until another round of Coal Island headlines needed to be told but she came back the next morning with the usual smile on her face and the same fingering of the biscuit and chocolate section.

'Eh, Fatihah,' she said as she handed me a packet of Kandos chocolate for kids, 'you one lying woman! You never tell me you got a boyfriend long time ago! Ya, I bump into Mrs Kumaran. She about your age what. Say she remember the time when you go hopping and skipping with one young Malay man. What happen to him, ah?'

So, I thought, she went digging. I hoped that Pong Pong would fly in, flap his wings and say that he had turned into a bat. I was in no mood to start talking about my youth and even if I was, Mrs Teng was not the person I wanted to say anything to. 'Oh, that was my cousin,' I said and made an excuse to visit the storeroom. There was no need to lie, of course. I had been in love once. His name was Faiz and he broke off our engagement before leaving the island and jumping off the Penang bridge. But that was forty two years ago and it belonged to a different life. I had no pain left for an early heartbreak and a lover's suicide. Still, I did not want to discuss my spinsterhood with a woman who absorbed sensation even when she was asleep.

Thankfully, the first case of bats inside a roof arrived the next day. Mrs Kumaran claimed that she had been awoken by screeches and loud scratching noises as if somebody was making a drawing with their fingernails on her ceiling. Pong Pong was immediately notified. A few people gathered at Mrs Kumaran's house that afternoon, including myself, because I couldn't bear the thought of not seeing the only known instance of human-animal communication on the island. The bat whisperer entered the premises dressed in a black cape and Japanese slippers. People started laughing, saying, 'Looks like we got our own Batman on Coal Island.' But Pong Pong was serious. He didn't smile or greet anybody and looked at the ceiling as though he could see what was going on inside it. Then he brought out a fluorescent orange whistle (I think he got it from the Beach Shop) and blew it.

Phreeeeet. He lifted his arms like a hawk about to catch a rat and brought them down again. Phreeeeet. He chanted, 'Olaoh. Olaoh. Olaoh.' Phreeeeet. He closed his eyes and when he opened them he said, 'They say they no want leave. They like it here. They have house and they feel warm.'

Mrs Kumaran jumped off her seat. 'Listen to me,' she shouted, 'you tell them that the house is mine! My husband didn't build it for bloody bats! Ask them to go to someone else's roof to feel warm and cosy! Cuddle up and shit and mate and do whatever it is they do inside *another* roof!'

The bat whisperer nodded. 'Okay, Mrs Kumaran,' he said,

'I go tell them'. Phreeeeet. Olaoh. Olaoh. Olaoh. Phreeeeet. He closed and opened his eyes. 'They ask if you got recommend another place. They no want make mistake again like last time,' he said.

The house went silent. People wondered if Mrs Kumaran would be heartless enough to move a family of bats into someone's home. She looked around the room and smiled. 'Well,' she said calmly, 'I'm happy that they're willing to compromise. I think I know just the place they'll like. Tell them they'll have a nice five star hotel.' She paused and we waited.

'Okay, Mrs Kumaran,' said the bat whisperer, 'they ready'.

She called Pong Pong to her and revealed the new location in a whisper that none of us could hear. Phreeeeet. Olaoh. Olaoh. Olaoh. Phreeeeet. 'They say,' Pong Pong announced, 'they go look see tonight.' We demanded to know which house had been selected for the bats but both Mrs Kumaran and the bat whisperer refused to tell us. We would have to find out ourselves.

I returned to the shop, amazed that Pong Pong could talk to bats and I wanted to know whether he could communicate with other animals too but before I could conduct my research, Mrs Teng came in, puffing on her asthma pump.

'What miracle, hah, Fatihah? You think so Pong Pong lying or he for real?' she said, wheezing and coughing in between her words.

'Looks real to me,' I said, 'the way he chanted and all that. We'll see lah. If Pong Pong is called to a house tonight then we know.'

Bats have lived on the island probably since it was created. They flap about at twilight, often flying as low as swallows, and hang from trees but sometimes they choose to live in houses. In the past, there had been a couple of cases of bats inside roofs and the pest control people were called. The bats were killed and it wasn't pleasant to have their spirits haunting homes. At least now we had a person who could talk to them and deal with the situation kindly.

'So, Fatihah,' Mrs Teng continued, 'to change subject. You really know how to hide thing ah. Hai. Hai. Hai. Why want to keep secret like this lah? That boy not your cousin, isn't it? Before everybody come to Mrs Kumaran's house, I go early to see her. She say he engage to you. Then he break your heart and go kill himself. Wah! Fatihah, so sorry all this happen. You still think about it?'

I couldn't believe she had not let my life go. The phone rang at that moment and even though it was just the bread delivery man arranging for an earlier time to bring his load in the next day, I kept him on the line for a full twenty minutes, going through with him the quantity and type of every bread and bun that I stocked in my shop. Mrs Teng lost her patience and attention, especially when she spotted Pong Pong outside fluttering his cape with his hands, like a bat in flight. She ran after him. I admired her energy and dedication in making sure that the island's stories were never neglected and, most of all, that they were kept alive through spreading. I didn't have much to hide. She did already know about my only relationship with a boy who, when we were together, said he liked my fat. It took me years to accept that Faiz had decided to stop living and I was touched that the final lines of his suicide note read: 'Fatihah, I'm sorry we never got to have a family. I'm doing this not because I want to make you unhappy but because I know that I never will.' I was glad to be remembered during his last moments on earth. After my broken engagement and Faiz's suicide, I worked for Abah in the shop. Ibu passed away a few years later and I was sad for a year but I was getting good at recovering what was habitual and carried on, with Abah, in making the shop the best on the island.

The morning after the bat whispering, a small crowd arrived at Mrs Kumaran's house. I locked up the shop and joined them. I wanted to know if the bats had moved and if there was going to be a fight. I imagined the new bat host saying to Mrs Kumaran, 'You sick bitch! How dare you?' The bats, it turned out, had left but no one was accusing Mrs Kumaran. 'Eh, eh,' people said, 'then where they go? Must ask Pong Pong.' The bat whisperer was summoned. He came with a cryptic face and only said, 'Bat give me message they going where they is needed.' No one was satisfied with his answer and we demanded an exact location. He said he didn't know. The crowd dispersed unhappily but a new respect had formed for Pong Pong. 'So he really got special gift,' people said, 'even though he gay.'

For days no one knew where the bats had gone. Soon, everyone started talking about other things such as Mrs Mano's latest vision in which the Virgin Mary had appeared to tell her about the Our Lady cake which, if baked with a pure heart, could cure all illnesses. My shop swarmed with people who came in to buy flour, eggs, butter, milk, cinnamon, raisins and chickpeas. 'Chickpeas?' I asked. 'Ya,' replied one customer, 'that one is the secret ingredient. This cake going to cure cancer.' I let them believe what they wanted to. After all, I was taking in quite a bit of money and people needed faith. While the island was busy making their godly goodies, I heard it. It was a dull, quiet scratching noise coming from the roof. I went upstairs and listened. So, the bats had chosen me. It's hard for me to name the feeling I had when I realized that living above me, like little buoyant guardians, was a group of winged animals that were breathing at the same time that I was when I was asleep. The years I had spent disbelieving in pets suddenly became void. There was life in my home even when I wasn't there.

I didn't tell anyone that the bats had moved into my roof. If they knew, Pong Pong would be called and I wouldn't have them anymore. For the first time in twenty years I sat on my bed, not to sleep. I looked up to the ceiling and said softly, 'Welcome. You know, you're the only ones I've allowed in here. I think we can be friends. Finally, something new has come.' They scratched the roof in reply.

I started closing the shop early to sit upstairs and talk to them. I wanted to tell them everything but everything was of the past and so I repeated the early stories of when Faiz and I were together, how he broke my heart and killed himself. But after a while, the bats stopped scratching the roof and I feared that I was losing them. When they became completely silent, I panicked. Then something clear came into my head. I said to myself, 'You gone mad or what? You think the bats care? How did you end up being alone and talking to bats about nothing? All the quietness became wild. You call this a life?'

Pong Pong came the next day and my roof returned to being empty. Mrs Teng was the first one to ask me. 'Oh, Fatihah,' she said, 'keep quiet again ah? How come you never tell us about it?'

'Because,' I replied, 'there's nothing to tell.'

For once, she was silent.